Secrets

OF

Willow Springs

BOOK 1
The Amish of Lawrence County Series

Tracy Fredrychowski

ISBN 978-1-7342411-2-9 (paperback)
ISBN 978-1-7342411-3-6 (digital)

All Bible verses taken from New Life Version Bible (NLV) and the New King James Version (NKJV)

Published in South Carolina by The Tracer Group, LLC
https://tracyfredrychowski.com

Contents

A Note about Amish Vocabulary

The language the Amish speak is called Pennsylvania Dutch and is usually spoken rather than written. The spelling of commonly used words varies from community to community throughout the United States and Canada. Even as I did research for this book, the spelling of some words changed within the same Amish community that inspired this story. In one case, spellings were debated between family members. Some of the words may have slightly different spellings, but all come from the interactions I've had with the people in the Amish settlement near where I was raised in northwestern Pennsylvania.

While this book was modeled upon a small Amish community in Lawrence County, this is a work of fiction. The names and characters are products of my imagination and do not resemble any person, living or dead, or actual events that took place in that community.

List of Characters

Emma Byler. A loveable teenager looking forward to her birthday and attending her first *singeon*. She loves her life in her Willow Springs and can't imagine being anywhere else. When she overhears her *datt* say her life will never be the same, she fears whatever secret he is keeping from her will change her life forever.

Jacob Byler. The overprotective *datt* to Emma. The secret he's kept for sixteen years has become more than he can bear and he tends to take out his anxiety about the future on Emma.

Stella Byler. *Mamm* to Emma and *fraa* to Jacob. Her calming manner helps Jacob come to terms with delivering on the promises he must keep for his late brother-in-law Walter.

Matthew Byler. The twenty-year-old *bruder* to Emma who has become somewhat of a loner since the love of his life, Sarah, moved to Sugarcreek.

Daniel Miller. The twenty-one-year-old English boy and best friend of Matthew. When his duty to his biological mother sends him to Sugarcreek to look for his long-lost sister, he discovers a secret the Byler family has kept hidden for way too long.

Samuel Yoder. The eighteen-year-old boy next door. Samuel has waited two years to share his secret with Emma.

Katie Yoder. Samuel's younger *schwester* and Emma's best friend.

Levi and Ruth Yoder. Owners of Yoder's Strawberry Acres and neighbors to Jacob and Stella.

Sarah Mast. When Sarah's *schwester* Susan dies in a buggy accident, she's sent to Sugarcreek to take care of her *schwester*'s *kinner* and struggles with coming to terms with her responsibilities to her family and her love for Matthew.

Nathan Bouteright. After losing his young *fraa* Susan, the forty-year-old widower finds peace in his sister-in-law, Sarah, as she helps him take care of his *kinner*.

Anna Mae Troyer. The sixty-year-old *schwester* to Jacob finds herself begging her brother to carry out the promises he made to her late *mun* sixteen years ago.

Chapter 1

The Hiding Spot

"A glad heart makes a cheerful face, but by sorrow of heart the spirit is crushed."

—Proverbs 15:13

(NLT)

June 2017

Emma sat in the far corner of her parent's porch protected from the rain and hidden from the watchful eye of her *datt*. Leaning her head against the back of the chair, she tried to remember when her *datt* started to act so strange. He told her again that morning that under no circumstances was she to go anywhere without him or her *mamm*.

Sitting back up in her chair, she petted Someday on his head and wrapped her arms around his neck and whispered. "I can always count on you to be glad to see me."

Listening to the sound of the rain on the roof was just what she needed to calm her anxiety over staying out of her *datt*'s way. It was just about as soothing as working in the garden. She loved the feel of the warm soil in her hands and enjoyed tending to the gardens around the farm. The purple and white pansies along the picket fence were in full bloom, and she smiled at how they looked as if they were welcoming the spring rain. Closing her eyes again, she leaned back and replayed the conversation she had had with her *datt* at breakfast.

"Do you know what today is?"

"A canning day," her mamm *said as she put a plate of pancakes in the middle of the table.* *"We have three baskets of strawberries waiting for us on the back porch."*

"That too, but it's June 17, and it's just thirty more days until my birthday."

She turned toward her datt. *"I thought you might let me go to the market with the girls this morning."*

"Didn't your mamm *just say you were helping with strawberries?"*

"Ja, but I thought just this once you might let me go."

"Well, you thought wrong."

She knew better than to argue and just went back to her breakfast, feeling defeated again by his sharp tone.

The sound of the sliding barn door startled her, and she opened her eyes and looked across the yard. Matthew, her *bruder*, was in the barn tending to a sick calf. He was standing in the doorway as if he was looking for a break in the rain to make it back to the house.

She leaned back and thought how rare it was to be enjoying such a long break from her Saturday chores. They had been making jam all morning, and the smell of strawberries was still thick in the air. They had just come upstairs from the basement kitchen when her *datt* came storming through the kitchen door. She hadn't even gotten a chance to pour a glass of meadow tea before her *mamm* shooed her outside.

Stella pulled a chair out so Jacob could sit down. She glanced to make sure Emma had left the room and grabbed Jacob's hand and started to rub it lovingly.

"What's the matter?" she asked as she handed him a glass of tea.

"I don't understand how three orders got mixed up, the lumber delivery delayed, and why Matthew has another sick calf."

"Let Kathryn worry about the orders, and Matthew will figure out what the problem is in the barn. You need to quit letting these little things upset you so."

He knew she was right, but it was getting harder and harder to control his anxiety. When silence fell between them, Stella looked into his eyes and saw the same fear she saw six months ago, when the letter and the newspaper article came from his *schwester* in Ohio.

"This has nothing to do with the orders, does it?"

He hung his head and started to rub the back of his neck with his free hand.

"I have a notion this has more to do with Emma's birthday than anything else. When she mentioned her birthday this morning, I saw that panicked look in your eyes. I pray *Gott* will give us direction and show us what we need to do. He won't let us down, Jacob. There's nothing we can do to protect Emma other than put our faith in the Lord. He gave her to us to protect, and we need to have faith that He'll help her with the choices she soon needs to make."

Jacob leaned back in his chair, closed his eyes, and said, "I know He'll watch over her, but we're running out of time. No matter how hard I try to keep her close, I think what I'm really doing is pushing her away. I promised Walter, before he died, I'd tell her the truth when she turned sixteen."

"Jacob, we knew this day would come, and I'm as worried as you are. But what good are we doing by forbidding her to leave the *haus*? When she turns sixteen and starts her *rumshpringa*, there's nothing we can do but let her make her own choices."

"What are you afraid of?"

"I'm afraid she won't want to stay with us once she learns the truth."

Stella leaned in closer and laid her head against his while she recited one of her favorite Bible verses, "Do not be anxious about anything, but in every situation, by prayer and petition, with thanksgiving, present your requests to God."

Emma felt protected in the corner of the porch where she couldn't be seen. Across the yard, she spotted her *bruder* again. Matthew was five years older and took care of the farm, while her *datt* tended to the furniture shop. Matthew kept to himself, and the only friend she knew he had was Daniel Miller from the feed store. She had been sure Sarah Mast would end up being her sister-in-law, but she moved to Ohio suddenly last year. Matthew never mentioned her name and spent most of his days in the barn with his calves.

As she continued to enjoy her solitude, she heard the clip-clop announcing her *schwester*'s wagon as it turned down the long driveway.

Her *datt*'s mood was getting worse, and she noticed the change in him every time she entered the room. Just yesterday, she asked her *mamm* again if he was upset with her about something, and her *mamm* just assured her she was just imagining it.

Lately, she sensed she frustrated her *datt* to no end. She often felt him glare at her, always followed by him rubbing his hand along the scar that lined his face from his temple to his chin. She wished she understood his sudden reaction to her, and she vowed to stay out of his way the best she could. She had to believe the scar on his face had something to do with it, but lately, no one could break through his icy, cold stare but her sweet *mamm*. Years ago, she tried to get them to explain the scar, but they told her it was doings of the past and nothing would be gained by talking about it.

As Emma rocked in her favorite chair, she suddenly remembered the strawberry flower Samuel Yoder had picked and quietly passed to her without a word yesterday. Him on one side of the row, and her on the other, their fingers often brushed as they reached to pick the ripest berry. On one of her last reaches, he slipped the little white flower into the palm of her hand. When she looked up, he acted like he had done nothing out of the ordinary.

As quickly as he passed the flower, he rolled one of his corny jokes off his lips. "What do you call a cow that has the jitters?"

She put the flower in her apron pocket without mentioning it and said, "I don't know. What do you call a cow with the jitters?"

"Beef jerky!" Samuel laughed at his own joke and got up and carried his full basket to the wagon at the end of the row.

No words were needed, and the silent connection and joyful way he had at making her laugh was all she needed. As soon as she got home, she placed the delicate small flower in her special memories box.

Samuel was two years older and was already attending Sunday night *singeons*. She smiled at the thought of being able to attend next month.Samuel's sister Katie, and her best friend, would turn sixteen two days after her, and they looked forward to going together. They had been best friends since they learned to walk and spent every spring picking berries and every summer playing in the creek. From the time they could carry a basket, they'd been crawling through the berry patches together.

The Yoders' farm butted up against their farm, dividing the two properties with a line of sugar maple trees. Emma and Katie's *mamms* had both grown up together and were best friends for as long as either of them could remember. Emma's parents had inherited the farm when her *doddi* died twenty years earlier. Emma's *datt* grew up in Sugarcreek, Ohio, and moved to Willow Springs to apprentice with *doddi* when he was seventeen. That was all Emma knew about her *datt*'s past. He never spoke of his childhood or any of his family in Holmes County and never about the scar on his face.

The rain had stopped, and the sun was starting to peek through the clouds when she heard the screen door slam. Shortly after, she saw her *datt* walk across the yard to the wood shop, she heard her *mamm*'s fingers tap on the window behind her, signaling for her to come back inside.

The next day, church was being held at the Mast Farm. Emma and her *schwesters* decided to walk instead of riding in the buggy. It was only two miles and a perfect morning for a walk. The sky was bright blue, with a few white puffy clouds sprinkled about. On their way, they stopped to enjoy watching a spring lamb frolic in the pasture as they stepped aside to let a buggy go around them. Once they turned off Mystic Mill Road and onto Willow Lane, they walked down the middle of the road with no care in the world. Emma loved to be outside and marveled at everything she saw.

Sap had stopped flowing months ago, but there were still a few sugar maple trees that had collection buckets on them. The pastures were green and lush from the spring rain, and a herd of black and white cows roamed through the pasture while they took no mind to the girls. The large, white barn adjoining the field had its big double doors to the hayloft open, and two cats sat on the edge of the door, watching the barnyard beneath them. Few cars traveled on the back roads of their Amish settlement, and they could enjoy their walk without worrying about traffic. The occasional humming of buggy wheels was the only thing that pushed them to the side of the road.

Anna and Rebecca were identical twins but had two completely different personalities. Their looks might be the same, but you could always tell them apart once they opened their mouths. They both had dark hair and bright blue eyes, the same color of the morning glories that grew alongside the barn, just like their mother's.

Once they got to the large, white clapboard farmhouse of Eli Mast, they got in line to go into the service. The petitioned walls that separated the kitchen from the living room had been removed, and benches were neatly lined up in rows facing each other. She sat in the second-to-the-last row right next to her best friend, Katie Yoder. On the other side sat Rebecca and Anna.

Once she was seated, she looked around the room for Samuel. He stood directly across from her on the other side of the room. There were more men than women in the twenty-two families that made up their church district, so some of the men had to stand during the service.

As the song leader started the first song from the *Ausbund* songbook, she could feel someone watching her. She looked around the room, and her eyes stopped on Samuel, just as he crossed his eyes, made a funny face, and turned away. She looked away, thinking that he couldn't have just made a face at her. She kept still, looking straight ahead while trying to concentrate on the words.

Just when she thought she'd been mistaken, she looked over at him, and he did it again. She put her hand over her mouth and tried to hide a giggle. Katie elbowed her, and her *mamm* turned in her seat to see where the laugh had come from. Katie saw what Samuel had done and turned toward Emma and then toward her *bruder* and gave them both a stern look. Emma purposely didn't look his way again until they started to sing the second song, the "Lob Lied."

Samuel told her a couple weeks ago that it was his favorite song. He explained how he found it amazing that every other Amish district throughout the country was singing the "Lob Lied" at the same exact time. She marveled that he was touched by the song and told him that it must make a beautiful sound in heaven.

When she lifted her head to look his way, she noticed he no longer needed to look at the words in the songbook and could sing it by heart just like she could. During the twenty-minute song, she caught him looking her way a few more times. That time, he made no funny faces as he was fully enjoying the slow song. This was her favorite part of the service, and it helped her ready her heart to hear the sermon that followed.

As soon as the service was over, she headed to the kitchen to help put moon pies on a platter to be served. Before she reached the kitchen, Samuel made a point to walk her way, and as he passed, he said, "Was that a giggle I heard?"

In a whisper, she said, "You know exactly what I found so amusing. Did you see the look I got from my *mamm*? I'm sure I'm going to hear more about that when I get home." She couldn't help but smile as she looked up at him.

He was at least six inches taller than her, and his crisp white shirt and starched black pants made him seem even taller. His face was tanned from working in his family's strawberry fields, and his boyish grin had her captivated. No matter what, she loved his playful disposition the most. Things at home were so tense lately, she looked forward to the fun banter they had with each other. Before he left to go help the men push the benches together to make tables, he asked if she was coming back to the *singeon* that evening.

Emma looked around to make sure no one had come up to them before she answered, "Once I turn sixteen, I'm certain my *datt* will let me go. But I don't dare ask before that. He's been moody, and I don't want to set him off."

"I'm sure he has his reasons for being so short. It takes a lot to run a business and a farm. My *datt* gets the same way sometimes,especially in the spring when the berries need picked."

He leaned in closer and whispered, "just so you know, I'll be glad when you can come."

As he walked away, he brushed his dark brown hair off his forehead and put his hat back on as he picked up a bench to help with the tables. He turned and winked at her as he walked away with a big grin on his face.

She couldn't help but smile at the interest he was showing in her. Her birthday couldn't get here fast enough.

Chapter 2

Strawberry Pie

The following Saturday, Matthew could hear the delivery truck downshift before it even turned in the driveway. His friend Daniel Miller had been delivering feed to the farm for a couple years, and they had become good friends. As it got closer, he put the pitch fork and shovel away and headed to the door.

"I bet you're glad it's stopped raining," Matthew said, as he walked out of the barn to meet Daniel.

Daniel extended his hand and gave Matthew a friendly handshake. "The rain stopped, the sun is out, and you're my last stop for the day."

Matthew looked forward to Daniel's deliveries, and even though he wasn't Amish, Matthew felt a connection to his English friend.

"I'm hungry. I was thinking about going to the sandwich shop on my way back into town. Are you up for a break?"

"Are you hungry or are you wanting to see Melinda?" Matthew replied.

Daniel dropped his head and started kicking a stone on the ground, trying to hide the smile that was spreading across his face. "A late lunch sounds good. How about you unload the feed while I wash up?"

Daniel had only arrived in Willow Springs for a short time when he found a friend in Matthew. Pennsylvania was so different than it had been in Ohio. He felt out of place, but Matthew made him feel like he could fit in. Daniel's father took a job with the Missionary Outreach Center in Pittsburgh and settled his family an hour north of the city in Willow Springs.

It didn't take long to unload the milk replacer and alpaca feed to the back of the barn where Matthew stored it. Before climbing back into the truck, he knocked the mud off his boots to wait for Matthew. He loved the Byler Farm; it was so different from the foster homes he had lived in before he was adopted.

The farmhouse had a huge wraparound porch that covered two sides of the house. The white clapboard structure and the baby-blue front door always looked like they had just been painted. There were four rockers lined up on the porch, ready for visitors, and he noticed huge ferns had been added to the porch since the last time he was there. He sawEmma move the rockers to sweep under them and lifted her hand to wave at him when she saw him.

Across the yard, Matthew's father was talking to a couple who had just stepped down from their brown top buggy. He wasn't sure how he felt about Mr. Byler. He rarely spoke to him and gave him the impression he didn't approve of their friendship. Matthew mentioned once his father didn't take too well to Englishers, and he was afraid their friendship would result in Matthew leaving his Old Order Amish Community.

Once Matthew climbed into the truck, Daniel pulled away from the barn and made his way down the driveway and toward town. Without saying a word, both men fell into a comfortable silence as they enjoyed the drive. The pastures on both sides of the road were turning a beautiful spring green, perfect for the sheep and cows grazing in them. As they approached Yoder's Strawberry Acres, Daniel slowed the truck down in anticipation of the traffic pulling in and out the farm.

Matthew noticed Katie was tending the roadside stand and Samuel was helping a customer load baskets of berries in the trunk of her car. This was a busy time for the Yoders, and he was glad the rain stopped so they could sell their strawberries.

Daniel smiled, as he stated, "I sure hope there's strawberry pie on the menu."

Matthew knew his friend long enough to know he had a sweet tooth a mile long, and any pie would do as long as it was served by Melinda.

"Samuel delivers berries to them every couple days, so I'm sure of it."

The mention of strawberry pie made Matthew start daydreaming about Sarah and the last time he saw her.

Last spring

Sarah had been in charge of cutting pies for the meal after church and was filling small plates when Matthew spotted her. Her dark blue dress and starched white *kapp* blended in with every other girl, but he could pick her out without ever seeing her face. Her dark, wavy hair fought to keep tucked beneath her *kapp*, and she was always fussing with the strands that tried to escape. Even though he was full, he had to go ask for a piece just to be near her. Out of the corner of her eye, she saw him coming. She quickly reached into her pocket to retrieve a small folded piece of paper. Looking to make sure no one had seen her she closed her hand around the note.

Luckily, as soon as he got close, the two girls that were working with her went to the kitchen for more plates.

"So, if I want a piece of the best pie, which one would you suggest?"

"If I were you, I'd stay away from the chocolate and head straight to the strawberry at the end of the table."

Matthew went to reach for a slice when he heard her whisper.

"Let me get it for you."

As she picked up the plate, she positioned the note in her hand so it would be hidden. Handing the plate to him, she hesitated long enough to make sure he felt the note and wouldn't let it fall to the floor.

Alarmed by what he felt he lifted his head to look at her. Her eyes told him he needed to take it quickly and not let on what she'd just done. Before he had a chance to say a word, she left him standing there, note in hand.

"Hey, have you heard a word I've said?"

Daniel was looking at him when he turned from the window.

"I'm sorry, I guess I was daydreaming. What did you say?"

"I was asking you what you found so interesting about those sheep."

"Absolutely nothing."

Before he knew it, they were pulling into the Feed & Seed to drop off the delivery truck in exchange for Daniel's truck. He'd been so busy in the barn, he didn't stop to eat and realized it was closer to supper than it was to dinner and he was hungry.

Matthew saw Daniel smile as they walked through the doors of the Haven Sandwich Shop. Daniel tipped his hat at Melinda when she looked his way.

She told them to take a seat anywhere, and she'd be right with them.

They slipped into a booth close to the counter and started to look over the menu.

"Are you going to ask her out soon? You can't keep spending your whole paycheck here just to talk to her."

"Her family goes to our church, and I've wanted to ask her father's permission before I call on her. Our youth group is starting back up the summer volleyball tournaments, and I am hoping she'll be there."

Matthew drifted again and thought if Sarah's *datt* had known they planned to get married, he might not have sent her off to Ohio. Their parents had no idea they'd been talking marriage and usually didn't know of a wedding until a few weeks before it was published at church. Had they known, they may have allowed her to return to Willow Springs by now.

"There you go again. What are you thinking so hard about today?" Daniel said as he turned his head just in time to see Melinda walk up to their table.

"Hello, Daniel."

Just hearing Melinda's sweet voice made Daniel's day.

"What can I bring you today?"

"I'm gonna skip a sandwich and go for a big slice of strawberry pie and a cup of coffee."

"How about you, Matthew, would you like pie as well?"

"No, I'll pass on the pie and take a hot ham and cheese and a root beer."

Melinda jotted down the order and headed to the kitchen.

The sandwich shop was a favorite stop for the locals. A small chalkboard sat on the sidewalk outside the front door listing the daily specials, and the aroma of freshly baked pies was an excellent way to entice people to come inside. The red checkered tablecloths and small oil lamps on each table gave the shop a welcoming feel. The owners an English couple, who lived upstairs, went out of their way, making sure everyone felt at home.

Melinda wasted no time delivering coffee and root beer to their table and said.

"It seems that the sunshine brought everyone out, every table is full. What has you two in town on a Saturday afternoon?" she asked.

Matthew was the first to speak. "Daniel claims he could smell strawberry pie from miles away."

Daniel smiled and nodded while adding cream and sugar to his coffee.

"The berries are so sweet. We can't make pies fast enough to keep the bakery case full." Just as she was about to say something else, one of her tables called her away for more coffee.

Before Melinda headed back to their table, she stopped to pick up Daniel's pie and Matthew's sandwich from the order window. After placing their food on the table and asking if they needed anything else, Daniel got enough nerve to speak up.

"Are you going to the church's volleyball tournament next Friday?" he asked.

Melinda smiled and looked Daniel right in the eye. "I haven't asked my father if I can go yet, but I am hoping he'll say yes."

"Well, just for the record, I hope he says yes too."

Melinda felt her face flush and turned when she heard the bell indicating her next order was up.

Matthew smiled as he teased his friend about his obvious crush on Melinda.

Daniel took a bite of pie and asked, "When am I going to be able to tease you about some pretty, young thing?"

Matthew's face turned serious as thoughts of Sarah crept back in.

"I doubt you'll get that opportunity anytime soon."

Matthew dropped his head and went back to eating his sandwich.

Chapter 3

The Delivery

Samuel closed the gate at the end of the driveway and turned to walk back to the storage barn. As he approached the barn, his *datt* was stacking baskets and talking to his *mamm*. He loved to watch his parents when they didn't know anyone was around. They had a way about them that told you they were as much in love as they were twenty years ago. He'd just turned eighteen and hoped someday he'd find that kind of love. Down deep, he hoped he'd find it with Emma Byler.

He knew his parents had overcome heartache with a number of miscarriages before and after his *schwester* Katie was born, but no one would ever know by the smiles on their faces. He'd just found out about the miscarriages after Katie discovered a family Bible listing all the *boppli*'s names and birth dates in her *mamm*'s hope chest. That kind of information was rarely shared, but Samuel felt his parents were relieved to be able to speak of their sadness.

Samuel cleared his throat and slapped his hat on the side of his leg to alert his parents of his presence. Ruth smiled and announced that supper would be ready at five, and she expected both of them to be cleaned up and at the table before it got cold.

"I'm going to ride into town and deliver these last baskets to the sandwich shop before it gets dark," Samuel said. "They'll not hold up until Monday, and Mr. Clamp said he'd be interested in whatever we had left at the end of the day."

Levi was proud that his son cared about the business. He could count on him to go out of his way to make sure their customers were taken care of.

"Go hitch up the wagon, and I'll get an invoice ready. Take a few of those extra baskets and drop them off at the Bylers before you head into town."

The way his *datt* smiled at him made him wonder if he knew how he felt about Emma. He'd just been given an excuse to stop and see her, and he was anxious to get going.

As Levi walked out of the barn, he handed Samuel an invoice for Mr. Clamp.

"The sun will bring everyone out on the roads, so I'd feel better if you go straight to the Bylers and to town and get back before it gets dark."

Samuel started to load the baskets in the wagon and said, "I'll be careful and won't waste time getting home. Have *Mamm* save me supper, and I'll eat when I get back."

Levi smiled at his son as he placed his hand on his shoulder.

"I'm not worried you'll waste time in town—my concern is you'll want to spend all your time at the Bylers."

Samuel turned his head away so he wouldn't see the smile on his face.

"Remember, son, I was eighteen once myself."

Samuel climbed into the wagon, turned it around, and tipped his hat to his *datt* as he left.

Saturday night meant the local college kids would be out joyriding. He knew he could handle the cart no matter what, but as fast as those kids drove their cars down Mystic Mill Road, it still worried him.

On the short ride to the Byler Farm, Samuel was able to enjoy the view as his thoughts were on the possibility of seeing Emma. As he slowed his wagon to turn into their driveway, a black pickup truck sped by so close, the hair on the back of his neck stood up. His wagon rocked, and the horse jerked at the quick movement. He'd never understand why the English felt the need to drive so fast and to be in such a hurry.

Don't they realize they'd enjoy so much more of life if they would just slow down? he thought.

Once he got the horse settled, he turned into the driveway and lifted his head just in time to see someone kneeling in the garden inside the picket fence. As he got closer, he could tell it was Emma. Her back was to him, but he knew it was her before he even got close enough to see her face.

Emma heard the clip-clop of a horse behind her and assumed it was one of her *datt*'s customers, so she didn't bother to turn around. She was cutting fresh spinach for supper when she heard the wagon stop behind her.

"You know, my *mamm*'s strawberry dressing would taste great on that spinach."

Emma knew instantly by the sound of his voice it was Samuel. She looked over her shoulder and said, "My thoughts exactly. And I made a fresh jar this morning. Are you here to tell me another one of your corny jokes?"

"I can come up with one if you want."

"*Nee* was just figuring."

Samuel didn't step down from the wagon but stayed put, in case her *datt* walked their way. From where he sat, he had a clear view of both the *haus* and the shop and felt safer speaking to her from where he sat. That far from the house, no one could hear what he was saying, but they definitely could see if he stood too close.

"I was hoping I'd get to see you. I wanted to ask you something."

Emma stood up and walked to the fence. She didn't know why she felt so nervous all the sudden.

He cleared his throat and acted like he was having trouble finding the words he wanted to say. "You turn sixteen in a few weeks, *ja*?"

Emma lifted her head and saw the hopeful look in his eyes. "*Ja.*"

"I wanted to wait until you could start going the *singeons* before I asked you this, but I just can't wait any longer."

"What do you want to ask me?"

"Can I start sending letters? I want to get to know you better."

"Samuel, we've been friends since we've been little. I'm sure you know all there is to know."

"I wanna know more."

She was about to tell him *yes* when she saw her parents walk out of the furniture shop. Her *datt* made her nervous, so she turned away from the fence and dropped back on her knees in the garden.

Without looking his way, she said, "I'd like that very much."

With a huge smile on his face, he picked up the reins and said, "Just what I wanted to hear. I best be delivering these berries to your *mamm* and be on my way."

Without thinking twice, he reached into the back of the buggy, picked up a berry, and tossed it her way.

Once she turned to look at him, he said softly so only she could hear, "You make me feel all warm and fuzzy, Emma Byler."

Just the sound of his voice and the words he'd just said warmed her heart. She turned her attention back to cutting spinach, but her thoughts were only on his words—*"You make me feel all warm and fuzzy, Emma Byler"*—words she vowed she'd never forget. She was all giddy at the thought of him wanting to write her. Her sister, Anna, had been receiving letters every Wednesday and was excited that she too would be able to talk to Samuel every week, even if it was in a letter. She was sure it was a sign he had intentions to court her.

After leaving the baskets on the front porch, Samuel turned the wagon around and headed to town. He fell into a soothing rhythm of his horse and with the sun shining on his face, he couldn't help but smile. It was getting closer to be able to tell Emma how he felt.

Before he knew it, he had reached the alley behind the Haven Sandwich Shop. He parked the wagon near the back door and spotted Daniel and Matthew climbing in Daniel's truck. Samuel whistled to get their attention, and Daniel drove his truck up beside the wagon. Matthew rolled down his window and was eye level with Samuel, who was still perched high on the wagon seat.

"When we drove past the farm a couple hours ago, you still had lots of customers. Was it a good day for picking?"

"It was a busy day, and I'm sure glad tomorrow is Sunday. I need a day off. As soon as I get the last of these berries delivered, I'm finished for the day."

He jumped down from the wagon and tied it to the hitching post. Turning toward Matthew, he asked, "I've been meaning to stop by and see how your calves are doing. You mentioned last week you had a few more sick. Have you been able to pull them through?"

Matthew's face turned to concern when he realized how long they'd been gone.

"I'm still trying to figure it out. I stopped and talked to the livestock vet to see if he had any clues, and he said he'd come out on Monday to take a look around."

"Speaking of which, I'd better get home. I need to check on things."

Samuel waved goodbye to his friends and knocked on the delivery door.

Within seconds, Mr. Clamp opened the door. "Samuel, your berries have been a huge hit this week. Mrs. Clamp can't make pies fast enough to keep the bakery case full. We'll be up late again tonight making pies for Monday. Bring them in, and I'll write you a check."

Mr. Clamp held the door open for him as he carried the baskets inside. He handed him the invoice and went back outside to the front of the wagon to check on his horse.

Down the street was the back entrance of the Restaurant on the Corner, a favorite hangout for the local college students. He heard a commotion and looked toward the restaurant. He spotted the same black truck in the parking lot that sped by him earlier. He heard loud voices and leaned around the horse to get a better view. From where he was standing, he could see what was happening, but the dumpster prevented anyone from seeing him. Two men and a woman were standing near the truck and must have assumed they were alone in the parking lot.

He stood still as he watched one of the men grab the woman by her hair and throw her to the ground. He felt like he was watching something in slow motion. The two men fighting, and the cries of the girl alarmed him. In his Old Order Amish upbringing, he was raised to drop everything to help a neighbor in crisis, but the thought of reaching out to break up a fight would be hard to explain to the bishop. He was taught to turn away and find a peaceful way to settle any dispute, but the cry for help from the girl was more than he could bear. He wished Mr. Clamp would come back outside.

The two men's voices were getting louder, and the girl was begging for them to stop. Just then, he saw one of the men slap the girl, and without thinking, he took off running toward them. Before he reached them, he heard a gunshot and froze in his tracks. He saw one of the men lying on the ground, and he stood staring at the man who fired the shot. The man now held the gun out, pointing it at the girl on the ground.

Samuel lunged toward the girl as the weapon went off, and then all went dark.

Chapter 4

Where's Samuel?

It was eight o'clock, and Levi was pacing in front of the sitting room window, he couldn't imagine why Samuel hadn't made it home yet. He had an uneasy feeling in the pit of his stomach that he just couldn't shake. Ruth and Katie were in the kitchen making cookies when Levi noticed the lights coming down the driveway. He knew before the car even stopped that something was terribly wrong. No one ever came to visit this late and especially in a car.

Ruth heard the car tires on the gravel driveway and rushed into the room as Levi headed to the door. Before the car had come to a complete stop, Levi had the front door open and was standing on the porch. He could tell by the color of the car and the lights on the top that it was a police car.

Levi had no idea what he was about to face, but he wanted to shield his family as much as he could.

"You and Katie stay in the house," he said as he walked out and shut the door.

An officer got out of the car just as Levi headed down the steps.

"Mr. Yoder, I'm Officer Koon from the Willow Springs Police Department. Is Samuel Yoder your son?"

"Yes, he is. Do you know where he is? He was supposed to be home hours ago," Levi asked as he walked closer to the officer.

Officer Koon took his hat off and said, "He was involved in an incident this evening behind the shops on Main Street. He saved a girl from being killed and was shot in the struggle. He's badly hurt and was airlifted to the University of Pittsburgh Medical Center."

Levi heard what the officer said, but it took a full minute for him to comprehend what was being described to him.

"Mr. Yoder, your son was very brave. He saved a girl tonight. He was in the parking lot behind the Haven Sandwich Shop when a fight broke out in a parking lot down the street. We're not certain of all the details, but we have apprehended the man who shot him. The young woman was not hurt, but there was another man that was killed in the same incident. You and your family will need to make arrangements to go to the hospital in Pittsburgh right away. Is there someone I can call or somewhere I can take you?"

Levi shook his head no and turned to return to the house.

Officer Koon hated that part of his job and shook his head as he climbed back into his car.

Levi opened the door to see Ruth and Katie holding onto each other, concern etched in their faces.

"Samuel was hurt and has been taken to a hospital in Pittsburgh. We need to make plans to leave right away."

"I'm not sure how long we'll be gone, so pack an overnight bag while I go call a driver."

The air was thick with fog, and he was in a daze as he walked off the porch to go to the phone shanty. He was trying to remember the number to the driver and hoped it was written down inside the phone shanty. Just then, he saw headlights coming down the driveway. The truck stopped beside him, and Jacob rolled his window down to speak to him.

"We heard about Samuel, and we're here to take you and Ruth to the hospital. Mr. Clamp called Daniel, Matthew's friend, to let him know he'd been shot."

"Daniel wasted no time picking us up and offering to drive you to Pittsburgh. The truck will only hold three people, so Daniel will take you and Ruth there now. Matthew and I will stay with Katie and will follow as soon as we secure a driver if you want."

Ruth was already on the front porch and heading down the steps when she heard Jacob explain how they were going to get to Samuel.

The look on Ruth's face broke Jacob's heart, and he could only imagine the turmoil she was going through, not knowing how severe Samuel's injuries were. Jacob spoke up first to ask Ruth if she wanted Stella to come with them.

"Oh, Jacob, that would be wonderful. Would you mind if Emma came? I'm sure Katie could use her."

Jacob didn't like Emma to leave the farm but couldn't see how it would hurt, especially with him close by. "Certainly, we'll all follow you as soon as our driver arrives."

Daniel was already on the phone to his father, asking him to come to the Yoder farm to pick up Jacob, Katie, and Matthew.

"It's all set. My father will be here shortly to take anyone that needs a ride to the hospital."

Once they were on their way, Levi didn't say a word the whole trip. He kept his head bowed deep in prayer, asking *Gott* to watch over his son. He knew whatever *Gott*'s plan was, they would need to accept it. *Kinner* were a gift from *Gott*, and the Lord and their Amish community would help them deal with whatever lay ahead.

Emma had gone to the living room after supper to read and had fallen asleep on the sofa. Stella went to wake her as soon as Jacob left with Matthew and Daniel. She knew Emma would be upset to hear about Samuel. Katie and Samuel were her best friends, and she'd want to know what was going on.

Stella sat on the edge of the sofa, looking at her youngest daughter. *How did she grow up so fast?*

The love she felt for this child was beyond anything she could describe. Her straight, blonde hair was coming loose from the confines of her *kapp,* and she couldn't help but smile at the hours they'd spent brushing it. She wished she could protect her from the events that were bound to invade their lives tonight and in the weeks to follow.

Stella brushed the hair away from her face and revealed a small mole on her left temple. Emma was always trying to cover the mole up with her *kapp*, and she was forever telling her it reminded her of a butterfly kiss and to stop trying to hide it.

Emma stirred and looked up into her *mamm*'s eyes. "Is something the matter?"

"Yes, I need you to wake up."

Emma wasted no time in sitting up. "You're scaring me, what's the matter?"

"I have some bad news to tell you."

As soon as Stella finished telling her all she knew, they sat quietly to wait for Jacob to return.

It wasn't long before Jacob, Matthew, and Katie came through the door with a man Emma didn't recognize. Jacob was the first to speak.

"Please get ready to leave. Mr. Miller is going to drive us to the hospital. Ruth wants you and Emma to come with us."

Without questioning him, they both got up to put on their shoes to get ready to leave.

Emma was trying to process everything that was happening when her *schwesters* came running down the stairs, asking what all the commotion was about.

"Samuel's been in an accident," Emma said.

Rebecca and Anna quickly turned their attention to their parents. Their *datt* started to go over the list of things they needed to take care of first thing in the morning.

Jacob turned to Matthew and said, "I want you to start organizing the neighbors to pick strawberries on Monday morning. If we don't get those berries picked, they'll spoil in the fields, and Levi won't be able to fill his orders. See to it that help is lined up and the stand opens on time."

As Matthew nodded at his *datt*'s instructions, Stella and Emma returned to the front room. Emma was choking up and knew it wasn't a good time to let her emotions get the best of her. Katie would need her strength, and Samuel would need her prayers.

The ride to Pittsburgh seemed to take forever. As they got closer, Emma could see the lights of the city. She'd never been to the city and felt a little scared. Mr. Miller was driving through the traffic with ease, and he didn't seem bothered by all the cars around them.

Emma leaned her head against the cold window and closed her eyes. It was only last week when Samuel slipped a flower into her hand and just that afternoon when he'd asked if he could write her. She could still see the smile on his face when she turned around after he'd thrown a strawberry at her. If her parents knew how deep her feelings were for him, they might not have let her come. It was better they thought she was there to comfort Katie and Katie alone.

Mr. Miller dropped them off at the entrance of the hospital and handed Jacob his business card with his phone number on it to use when they needed a ride back home. Emma had never been to a hospital and was not prepared for the array of lights and activity that surrounded the entrance of the building. In the past ninety minutes, life seemed to turn upside down, and she wasn't sure she was strong enough to face what might be ahead.

Emma reached for Katie's hand, and they both trembled as they walked through the doors together. The sights and smells of the sterile environment were all so new, and Katie leaned over and whispered how scared she was.

"I know. I am too."

Once they reached the information desk, the woman behind the counter looked up and asked who they were looking for.

Jacob told the receptionist he was looking for Samuel Yoder. The receptionist typed the name into her computer and directed them to the family surgical floor waiting room. She told them he was in surgery and a doctor would come and speak to them when they had something to report.

Jacob led the girls through the hospital and to the elevator. He knew it was going to be a long night and was anxious to find Levi and Ruth.

Chapter 5

Memories

The waiting room was filled with families all huddled around each other, most whispering within their small groups. The television in the corner caught Emma's eye as she tried not to stare at the sparsely dressed woman on the screen. Jacob led the girls to the corner of the room once he spotted Levi and Ruth. "Emma, did you hear a word I said?" Katie asked.

Emma turned toward Katie so her back was to the television and away from the distraction. "I'm sorry I didn't hear what you said. What is it? Do you need something?"

"Look at my *mamm*. She looks so scared."

Tears started to well up in Emma's eyes as she looked at Ruth. She could feel her pain from across the room and wasn't sure if the emotions that she was fighting were from seeing Ruth or the fear she felt by not knowing if Samuel was going to be all right.

Katie whispered to Emma, "You don't fool me, I know full well you and Samuel have eyes for one another. I haven't been your best friend for the last fifteen years to not know you're in love with my *bruder*."

"Shh, no one must know, especially my *datt*. If he knew, he'd never let me be here with you."

"Why?" Katie asked.

Emma lowered her voice and leaned into Katie as she whispered, "He's very protective, and if he knew, he might not let me come visit or help at the strawberry stand. I'm not sure what his problem is lately, but he won't let me go or do anything. It's like he's afraid someone will take me or something."

They walked across the room to where Levi and Ruth sat, and Emma heard her *datt* say, "I hate hospitals. Just the smell brings back awful memories."

She wondered what he meant by that, but before she could question him, a doctor dressed in green scrubs stood in the doorway calling for the Yoder family.

"Here," Levi stated as he stood up and started walking toward the doctor.

"Stay there," the doctor said as he walked to him. "Mr. Yoder, I am Dr. Hallman. I treated your son when he came in tonight. I just learned he's still in surgery, and I wanted to come and speak to you about his condition."

"Thank you. We haven't heard a single word about him since we've been here," Levi stated.

"Let's go into the consultation room next door so we can talk in private, and I'll tell you all I know."

"Can our friends come? It would be easier if they heard what you have to say so we don't have to repeat everything."

"Of course, follow me." Dr. Hallman turned and headed for the door.

The room was small, and Emma felt Katie's fear as she held her hand. They stood near the window to let their parents and Dr. Hallman sit down in the chairs around the table.

Dr. Hallman cleared his throat and began, "This is what I know from the report I got from the first response team. Your son threw himself in the line of fire to save a young girl. When he did that, he was hit in the right shoulder.

"Normally, a gunshot wound to the shoulder is not life threatening, but the bullet hit the subclavian artery beneath his collarbone, and he lost a lot of blood. He was in shock when he arrived and is in surgery now, trying to repair the artery and stop the bleeding. He also had a nasty bump on the back of his head.

"We assume the jolt of the gunshot threw him backward, and he hit his head on the ground. He was very lucky the firehouse was right around the corner. The EMTs had just returned from a call and heard the gunshot and ran to him immediately. They undoubtedly saved his life. Otherwise, he would have bled to death."

Levi reached for Ruth's hand as they both gasped at the news. Just as Levi started to ask what Samuel's chances were, the door opened and another doctor in scrubs stood in the doorway.

"Mr. and Mrs. Yoder, this is the surgeon that's been taking care of your son. This is Dr. Jennings."

Levi and Jacob stood to greet the doctor.

"No, please stay seated," he said. "He's out of surgery and is being stabilized in recovery. I was able to stop the bleeding and repair the artery. The bullet passed through his shoulder and exited through his scapula. He has severe damage to his collarbone and scapula. We can't be sure if any or how much nerve damage was done until he is awake and stable."

Ruth quickly asked how long it would be before she could see him. "He'll be in the ICU for at least twenty-four hours. I would suggest you all go home and get a good night's rest and come back tomorrow evening. By then, he should be stable enough to have one visitor at a time for a few minutes."

Taking a tissue from her purse, she wiped her eyes and looked at Levi, hoping he would not make her go home without seeing her son.

Dr. Jennings asked if anyone had any questions before he left and told them how they could reach him if they had any concerns about Samuel's recovery.

Jacob waited for the doctors to leave before saying, "There's no sense in all of us staying. We heard the doctor. There's nothing we can do until tomorrow. I'll go call Mr. Miller and ask him to turn around and come back for us. I can see Ruth has no intention of leaving the hospital tonight."

Levi nodded as he stood.

Katie ran and knelt at her *mamm*'s feet.

"He just has to be all right. I can't bear the thought of him not getting better."

"I know, my dear, we all feel the same way," she said as she stroked the back of Katie's head.

Emma was biting her lip as she struggled to keep it under control. Inside, she was silently praying for Samuel and his family. Everything was so scary; she never had someone she cared for so deeply be hurt so badly.

Jacob left the small room to go call for Mr. Miller as Levi, Ruth, and Stella huddled together to comfort each other.

As Jacob walked out into the hallway, he had the urge to run as fast as he could to escape the smell of the hospital. The sights, the sounds, and the smells all brought back a flood of memories he tried hard to bury. The scar on his face was a constant reminder that his dark secret would soon have to be revealed. If he hadn't had faith in the Lord, he might not have been able to control his emotions for the last fifteen years. Just hearing the doctor reveal the circumstances of Samuel's accident had him breaking out in a cold sweat.

Will I ever be able to escape the nightmare that haunts me, or is history going to repeat itself right before my eyes? he thought.

Jacob found a phone at the information desk and dialed Mr. Miller to return for them. Then he went outside for a breath of fresh air. As he leaned up against the wall of the large brick building, he closed his eyes. He remembered it like it was yesterday. It was an evening much like this one that changed his life forever. He could still remember hearing the cries of a baby and the look of terror on the young girl's face as he lay on the ground at the end of his *schwester's* driveway.

Jacob had been gone too long, so Stella went to look for him. She found him standing outside the entrance of the hospital.

"Jacob, I was worried when you didn't come right back. What's the matter?"

"It's this hospital. It's stirring up crazy memories."

"I could tell by the look on your face you were upset. You've not set foot in a hospital in a good long time."

Jacob hung his head and allowed Stella to lean in close to comfort him.

"I can't stop thinking that I can't protect her much longer. I've tried to keep her on the farm, but with her birthday coming up, I'm afraid her life is about to change forever."

Stella knew that this day would come but didn't realize that their visit to a hospital would have this kind of effect on him. She was as worried and upset as he was but knew all she could do was put her trust in the Lord and know He would guide them to do the right thing.

Emma and Katie walked to the elevator after saying their goodbyes to her parents. Katie wanted to stay, but her *mamm* convinced her that she was needed at home to run the strawberry stand. She was sad to leave but was proud her *datt* trusted her to take care of the stand while he was away.

Emma saw her parents leaning up against the hospital wall as she walked through the front doors. They both looked sad and thought they both must be feeling the pain Ruth and Levi were experiencing.

Emma was just about to reach out and touch her *mamm*'s shoulder when she heard her *datt* say her life was about to change forever. She stopped in her tracks, and a chill ran down her spine, she felt an overwhelming sense of dread come over her.

Just then, Jacob saw Emma standing behind Stella and knew she'd heard him. She started to question him about what he meant, but all he said was, "Not now, Emma," and turned to walk back into the hospital. They all followed him.

It wasn't long, and Mr. Miller pulled up to the front doors, and Jacob motioned to them that it was time to go.

Her *datt* sat in the front seat, telling Mr. Miller what the doctors had said, as Emma sat in the back looking out the window. She couldn't wait to get out of the city and back to the peace of the farm.

What did he mean by saying my life was about to change? She closed her eyes and prayed that *Gott* would help her deal with whatever changes her parents were talking about.

Katie tapped on her arm to get her attention and whispered, "Do you think your parents will let you help me at the stand on Monday? I'm going to need help."

"Before we left, *Datt* told Matthew to organize some of the neighbors to help pick strawberries on Monday. Matthew's going to get everything taken care of after church today."

"I'm sure everyone will have questions about Samuel. I hope we hear something before then," Katie said.

Stella turned to the girls and said, "You'll be staying with us until your parents return. You can stay in Emma's room, and you can wear one of her dresses to church today."

"*Denki*, I hadn't even given a thought to being home alone. I have the bag I packed when I thought we might be in the city for a few days, so I am all set."

Stella leaned her head up against the window as she looked at the back of Jacob's head. She worried their visit to the hospital would sour his mood for days. There had to be a way to make the news they had to share with Emma easier. Maybe they weren't giving her enough credit and she'd be fine.

After Emma had overheard their conversation, she was sure she'd be asking more questions. In just a month, they would be forced to give her the answers she deserved. Then it would be up to her on what she wanted to do, and nothing they could say would matter.

Stella looked over at Emma and smiled. Her daughter was turning into a woman right before her eyes, and she wasn't sure she was ready. She couldn't imagine her life without Emma in it and hoped she'd never have to find out. July seventeenth would be there quick enough, and she vowed to make the most of the last few weeks she had of Emma's childhood.

Chapter 6

Sunday

The house was quiet when they returned home.

"I see the light on in the barn. I'm going to go see if Matthew needs my help," Jacob said as he grabbed his barn jacket from the peg by the back door.

Stella reached for the tea kettle as she walked to the sink to fill it. "I won't be able to sleep, so no sense in going to bed now. Would you girls like to join me for a cup of tea?"

"Sounds nice," Emma said as she pulled out a chair to sit down and patted the seat beside her for Katie to join her.

"Mrs. Byler, do you think I should've stayed at the hospital? *Mamm* was so upset when we left."

"She's worried, but she'll do better once she sees your *bruder*. You heard the doctor—there's nothing any of us could have done until he gets out of the ICU. The best thing you can do for your parents is to make sure the stand opens and get those strawberries picked so they don't go to waste."

"I just feel so helpless."

Emma put her arm around her shoulder and said, "We'll round up all the girls at church this morning and see who can help at the stand for a few days. Hopefully, we can gather up enough help to get all the berries picked by noon."

Emma stood and walked to get a pen and paper out of the drawer by the back door as she continued to make plans for securing enough help.

Stella smiled. She could always count on Emma to take charge. Whether it was organizing a bake sale or helping a neighbor in need, she was always the first to step up and take charge.

Making a list of what needed to be done took their minds off Samuel, and before they knew it, they were engrossed in to-do lists.

Jacob found Matthew in the barn, sitting in the middle of a stall holding a calf's head in his lap.

"Not another one?"

"*Ja*, I'm afraid so. I don't understand what the problem is. I've tested the feed and double-checked with the vet to make sure I'm giving the correct dosage of medicine. I just don't understand what the problem is."

"I'm not buying any more calves until I get this under control," Matthew said. "The vet said he checks every calf when they're brought in and thinks the issues start after they come here."

Matthew pushed the dead calf off his lap and stood up to face his *datt*.

Jacob opened the stall to let Matthew out and turned around to count the existing calves in the stall across the hall.

"You only have two left of that last lot," Jacob said. "Do you think we should move them to the small barn out back so we can disinfect these stalls?"

"I thought about that, but with the alpacas in that barn, I would hate to spread anything to that area of the farm. These two are already starting to show signs of being sick."

Mathew took off his hat and slapped it on his thigh as he said, "I've been buying calves for two years now and never had this much trouble. It's only been the last three lots. I asked Johnny at the sale barn if someone new has been bringing livestock in, and he said just old man Smitty, like always."

Jacob walked over and leaned on the stall where the calves were lying in the corner.

Matthew put his hat back on and reached for the wheelbarrow to take the dead calf out of the barn.

"I walked all over the sale barn last Friday and couldn't find any area that wasn't clean and dry."

"Who else is buying?" Jacob asked.

"No one that I know of. I've purchased all that came up for sale the last few months. They all seem healthy when I load them up, and it's not until a day or two later I start seeing signs of sickness."

"Well, there's not much more we can do here. What's left to do before we get cleaned up for church?" Jacob asked.

"I told Rebecca I'd take care of the alpacas and feed the chickens since she was up late getting pies ready for church."

"You take care of that calf, and I'll do Rebecca's chores," Jacob said.

Matthew loaded the calf into the wheelbarrow and took it to the pit out back to burn when he got back from church. Farming wasn't always easy, but it was what he loved, and he'd continue to work to get to the bottom of this. He liked buying bottle calves to raise until they were weaned and ready for pasture. He spent the spring and fall planting soybeans to dry and sell to the Feed & Seed, and his calves were an excellent way to earn money between tending to the fields.

As he walked past the far side of the barn, he couldn't help but notice the sweet smell of lilac. The bushes were in full bloom and reminded him of Sarah. The sun was coming up over the horizon, and the smell of lilacs took him back to a morning just like this last year.

Spring of last year

Sarah passed him a note on Sunday, asking him to meet her on Friday at seven o'clock. They were to meet at their favorite spot near the cluster of lilac bushes by the covered bridge. She said she had something to tell him and she must do it in person. He'd fallen in love with Sarah, and they had just started to make plans to spend their lives together. When Friday morning came, he quickly finished his chores and hooked the wagon to his horse, anxious to see her. He was a few minutes early when he got to the covered bridge and had just enough time to get down from the wagon and pick a bouquet of lilacs.

Promptly at seven, he heard the clip-clop of a buggy echoing across Willow Creek. He wouldn't be able to see if it was her until the buggy came to a stop and turned right to cross the covered bridge. Not many people traveled on the back roads so early in the morning, so it was unlikely anyone would see them.

When she stepped down from the buggy, she was wiping her eyes. She didn't wait for Matthew to come closer before she ran and wrapped her arms around him, burying her head in his shoulder. He'd never been this close to her before, but it felt right holding her in his arms.

Sarah pushed herself back away from him and said, "I'm sorry."

Matthew lifted her chin with his finger and looked in her eyes. "You never have to apologize for letting me hold you. Now, tell me what has you so upset?"

"My *datt* is sending me to Ohio to help my brother-in-law look after the *kinner*. They're struggling since Susan died, and I have no idea how long I'll be gone."

Matthew wrapped his arms around her and let her cry on his shoulder. If he ever had any doubt she was the one he was meant to marry, it was all gone at that very moment. She felt so natural in his arms.

"We'll make it work. I'm sure the *kinner* need you more than ever right now. If it's *Gott's* will you go to Ohio, then so be it. We have a lifetime to be together, and sometimes you have to go where He leads you."

Sarah looked up and couldn't believe it may be months before she'd get to see him again. As their eyes met, he placed his hand behind her head and slowly pulled her closer to him. He softly kissed her lips and breathed in her sweet smell, some from the smell of the lilacs and some from the mist of the morning dew that lay on her *kapp*.

He moved his mouth to her ear and whispered, "I love you, my sweet Sarah, and when you return, I'll make you my *fraa*."

Sarah laid her head on his shoulder and wrapped her arms around his middle, not wanting to release the hold he had on her.

She hoped she could hold on to this memory for the long months ahead.

Matthew didn't want to let her go and lifted her chin to kiss her one more time. The taste of her lips sent shivers down his spine and only made his hold on her even tighter.

The memory of holding Sarah still made his heart skip a beat as he realized it had been a year since they met on that spring morning. He ached to understand why she hadn't sent a letter, letting him know how he could reach her. He tried to speak to her *datt*, but he was a hard man to warm up to. Her family didn't know about their relationship, and he didn't think it was his place to tell him without her knowledge.

The sound of his *datt*'s voice startled him and made him realize he'd been daydreaming again. He needed to snap out of all this daydreaming and figure out what was going on with his animals.

In the house, the twins, Emma, and Katie were busy setting the table for breakfast, as Stella was at the stove making scrambled eggs and bacon. Stella turned around and set a hot pan of biscuits on the table, just as Jacob and Matthew came in the back door.

"We'll have breakfast on the table in just a few minutes. You have enough time to wash up before we sit down," she stated.

Katie was trying to not get in the way as the three girls moved in complete harmony with each other as they set the table.

That was the one thing Katie missed about not having *schwesters*—the closeness they all had and how they all worked together made her yearn for a bigger family. She held her breath, trying not to cry, thinking if Samuel had died, she'd be left as an only child.

Emma saw her wipe her eyes with the back of her hand and reached to pull her into the living room.

"What is it?" she asked.

"I think the last eight hours are getting to me. So much has happened, and we still don't know how bad Samuel is. I hope my parents find a way to give us some news today."

"I'm sure they'll try, but for now, all we can do is concentrate on taking care of the strawberries. Your *datt* is counting on you, so keep that in mind."

Emma tucked some of her loose hairs back under her *kapp* and yawned as she said, "I think our biggest challenge will be staying awake at church."

Katie smiled as she heard Stella call them to the breakfast table. Once they all sat down, Jacob bowed his head for a silent prayer and kept his head lowered longer than usual.

Emma used the time to say an extra long prayer for Samuel. She wanted to see him smile, only then would she know he was going to be okay.

Jacob cleared his throat to signal the end of his prayer.

Emma had to fight to keep her eyes open and felt herself nodding off a few times during the service. Once the final sermon was finished, she wasted no time going outside to splash cold water on her face. She couldn't shake the anxiety she felt at overhearing her *datt*'s comment at the hospital and the worry she had for Samuel. Both were exhausting to her. At that point, all she wanted to do was go home and take a nap. But before that could happen, she needed to round up some girls to help them at the stand tomorrow.

As she turned the corner, Katie was already surrounded by a group of their friends asking questions about Samuel's accident. She didn't have anything different to tell them than what had already been announced, but it felt good knowing they were concerned about his well-being.

Emma took out her sign-up sheet and had all of the time slots filled within a few minutes. It was times like this when her *g'may* came together to help each other that she knew she'd never leave the folds of her Amish community.

Across the yard, Matthew gathered a group of men and was setting up times for help with deliveries. Once they all had everything organized, they went about helping with lunch.

The lunch meal was barely over when her parents gathered them up to go home. The buggy ride back home was silent. It usually was filled with lively conversation about what was going on with their neighbors, but that morning's ride was solemn. It wasn't long, and they were making their way down the hill that led to the farm. As they turned into the driveway, Emma noticed how pretty the flowers looked. The early afternoon sun was reflecting off the purple and white flowers along the fence.

As they passed the row of spinach, she remembered her short conversation with Samuel just yesterday. *"You make me feel all warm and fuzzy, Emma Byler."*

Those were the last words he'd spoken to her, and she fought to swallow the lump in her throat at the memory.

Just then, she saw Mr. Miller's van parked in front of the furniture shop. He was standing outside, leaning on the van, and started to walk to the buggy as her *datt* pulled up close to the porch. He handed Matthew the reins and stepped down from the buggy.

"Put the horse away while I talk to Mr. Miller."

After Stella and the girls had gotten down, Matthew drove off, and they all turned to Mr. Miller.

"I just got word from Levi that Samuel is out of recovery and in ICU. He said it'll be days before they know the extent of damage to his shoulder. He also said that the doctor is concerned with the bump on his head and will talk to them more about it when he comes in for rounds this morning. I told Levi you were getting the neighbors to help in the fields tomorrow, and he didn't need to worry about them."

"I can't thank you enough for driving out here to deliver that message," Jacob said.

"It's no problem, and when you need to go back, you just let me know."

At that, Mr. Miller turned around, climbed into his van, and drove away.

Once inside, Jacob instructed the girls to go take a nap, and Stella and he did the same.

Chapter 7

The Mystery

On the kitchen table laid a stack of books Matthew checked out from the library about animal health. He picked one of them up and headed to the porch. He picked up where he left off, looking for any clues he could find. He ruled out every common sickness and was about ready to give up when he started to read the chapter about poison.

The symptoms matched what he had been witnessing for months. His calves fell ill within a few days of arriving on the farm. The local vet had cleared the auction barn and was certain whatever was causing the problem was contained there on the farm. What really had him stumped was why the alpacas didn't seem affected by whatever was making the calves sick.

He stopped and reread the symptoms of lead poising. Diarrhea, excessive salivation, tremors, and loss of appetite all pointed to lead poisoning; but how could that be? The book warned of old car batteries and lead paint, neither of which was on the farm. He set the book aside and started to walk out to the barn. He was anxious for his *datt* to wake up so he could discuss what he had read.

In the meantime, he went to go check on the last two calves. As he entered the stall, he was too late as both calves were already dead and lay in the corner of the stall. He threw his hat on the ground and slammed the stall door and headed for the wheelbarrow.

In the house, Jacob tossed and turned as a nightmare had interrupted his afternoon nap. The sound of a *boppli* crying and a bright light shining in his face made him sit straight up in bed. It only took him a few seconds to realize it was a dream and quietly got out of bed, trying not to disturb Stella. He walked over to the window and saw Matthew carrying another calf out of the barn. He had to help him figure out what the problem was, but he had so many other things on his mind, he just couldn't think straight.

He sat in the rocking chair next to the window and laid his head back, trying to make sense of the dream he had just had. The stress of receiving letters from his *schwester*, Samuel's accident, and the dead calves were all wearing on him. He started to pray, not realizing he was talking out loud.

"*Gott*, please help me find the strength to speak to Emma. Help me find the words to tell her how much we love her and that we only did what we thought was best. Give her the guidance she needs to make one of the hardest decisions she'll ever have to make. Amen."

Stella felt him get out of bed and was standing behind him as he finished his prayer. She placed her hand on his shoulder, and he reached up and pulled her onto his lap. She nuzzled her head into his shoulder as she whispered that *Gott* was with them and would see them through this. Jacob lifted Stella's chin and kissed her ever so softly. At that moment, they pushed away all the stress from the last couple months and found comfort in each other's arms.

In the room down the hall, Emma and Katie woke up from their naps and were talking about Samuel. Katie was anxious to speak to her parents and to see Samuel.

By the way the sun was shining through the window, Emma could tell it was at least five o'clock, and her stomach was telling her it was time for supper.

She stood to iron out the wrinkles in her dress with her hands and said, "Let's go see about supper. It'll keep our minds occupied while we wait for my parents to wake up. Maybe Rebecca and Anna have started to put something together, and we can help them finish up."

As they went down the steps and into the kitchen, the twins had already set the table and heard them discussing that night's *singeon.* Rebecca stood up and told both girls to sit down while she went to the counter to pour them both a glass of lemonade.

Anna looked Katie's way and said, "While you were sleeping, Mr. Miller stopped back and delivered a message from your parents. He said they ran a CAT scan and didn't see anything that alarmed them. They said he still hasn't woken up, but they have been able to see him, and he is resting comfortably."

Katie was relieved and thanked Anna for the message.

"I wonder why the bump on his head has them more concerned than his shoulder," Emma stated.

"Mr. Miller seemed to think they were concerned that a concussion could cause memory loss," Rebecca said.

Just as Rebecca handed both girls a drink, Matthew walked in the back door. His face was etched with worry as he pulled out a chair and sat at the table.

He looked at Katie as he said, "I assume the girls told you about the message Mr. Miller delivered?"

"*Ja* they did, and we were just talking about it."

Rebecca and Anna both headed to the counter and started to pull cold cuts and leftovers out of the refrigerator to heat up for supper.

At the sound of the chatter in the kitchen, Jacob stated, "By the sounds of it, everyone has woken from their naps. Let's head downstairs. I need to talk to Matthew about those calves."

Trying to lighten the mood, Jacob stood quickly, and Stella fell off his lap and was laying on the floor, looking up at him, and smiled.

"What are you smiling about, my lovely *fraa*?"

"I remembered the first time we met. You knocked on the door just as I was opening it to go feed the chickens. Do you remember?"

"I certainly do, and if I recall correctly, you dumped a whole bowl of watermelon rinds at my feet when you bumped into me. I was a skinny kid, and you knocked me down when you came barreling outside." Jacob smiled as he looked at his *fraa*.

"I remember your face turning as pink as that watermelon when you realized what you'd done. And to make matters worse, when I stood up to help you pick them up, you slipped and fell right on top of me as we both tumbled down the steps."

"Do you remember the look on your *mamm*'s face when she came to the door only to see you lying on top of me at the foot of the stairs?" Stella smiled at the memory.

"I also remember after that you avoided me for weeks, and it took another couple months for you even to look my way. Looking back, I can say you fell for me the first time you saw me," Jacob said.

Stella laughed as she said, "If my memory serves me, I think it was you who avoided me. It took you months to join us for dinner."

As he started to head to the door, he said, "That may have been so, but right now, my stomach is not turning down any dinner invitations."

Just as Rebecca and Anna set the last of the leftovers on the table, both of her parents came down the steps. Jacob stopped at Emma and Katie and asked if they had a good nap.

Emma was the first to speak and was touched by the tenderness in his voice.

"I did, and *denki* for allowing us to take such a long nap. Mr. Miller stopped by again while we were sleeping and left a message about Samuel."

Katie spoke up and repeated the message as they all sat down at the table. Jacob bowed his head, and everyone followed until he cleared his throat, and they began to pass the dishes around the table. Jacob was the first to speak as he turned to face Matthew, who was seated to his left and directly across from his *mamm*.

"I saw you carry out another calf this afternoon. Was that the last one?"

Matthew finished swallowing and spoke up, "*Ja*, and I think I may have figured something out. I borrowed an animal health book from the library last week and had been reading through it, trying to come up with what might be the problem. I had just about given up when I turned to the chapter that talked about lead poisoning."

Jacob immediately stood up, grabbed his hat off the hook by the side door, and hollered at Matthew to follow him. The girls all looked at Stella, waiting for an explanation of what had just happened.

"I'm not sure what that's all about, but let's finish eating. If he wanted us to go with him, he would have told us to follow him."

Rebecca stood up and looked out the kitchen window to see where they were going.

"It looks like they are going to the barn. Do you think I should go with them?"

"*Nee*, as I said he'll call for us if we're needed. Now sit down and finish your supper," Stella said.

Rebecca didn't like not knowing what was going on. She was afraid that whatever was affecting the calves would somehow spill over to her three alpacas. She had a lot of time and money invested in those alpacas and couldn't bear the thought of them getting sick too.

Matthew had a hard time catching up to Jacob and didn't understand what got him so worked up. Jacob was headed to the back of the barn and into the workroom where the pump and generator were stored. He was frantically moving things out of the way to uncover something to show Matthew.

"As soon as you said lead poisoning, I knew exactly what the problem was. This barn is over one hundred years old, and the pipes leading from the well are lead. Where have you been getting water to mix the calf milk from?"

Matthew sat right down and put his head in his hands as he answered, "From the spigot on the other side of this room. The pipe that leads from the new alpaca barn broke a few months ago when Daniel got the delivery truck stuck in that early snowstorm. I'd been waiting for the ground to thaw and dry up before I fixed it correctly.

"I got busy planting the fields and didn't give it another thought once the weather got warmer. I never worried too much about it because I knew this well was still working. That explains why Rebecca's alpacas never got sick and why it seemed to come on all of a sudden."

"Son, these things happen. I should have replaced these pipes years ago and turned the water off for good to these pipes. This is as much my fault as anything," Jacob said. "Come on, son, let's go finish our supper and tell the girls what we've figured out."

"Rebecca has been so worried about those alpacas. She'll be relieved we finally have answers. That explains why nothing the vet was doing was helping. You were continually feeding them poisoned water."

Matthew stood up and brushed off his pants with the back of his hat and followed him to the house. As they both came in the back door, all the girls were still sitting at the table, anxiously waiting for their return.

Stella was the first to speak up.

"Jacob, your supper is cold. Let me heat it back up for you."

"Don't bother. Just pour me a hot cup of coffee, and I'll be good."

Matthew pushed his plate away once he sat back down.

"Son, not eating isn't going to bring those calves back. Now that we know what the problem is, you have some repairs to make to that barn before you buy any more calves."

"You're right, and those pipes are the first to go," Matthew said as he pulled his plate back in front of him.

Rebecca looked at Matthew and asked, "What did you figure out? Are my alpacas in danger of whatever killed the calves? Do we need to move them to another farm until repairs are done on the barn?" Rebecca talked so fast, her *datt* told her to slow down.

"I'll answer your questions one at a time as soon as you bring me a piece of that cherry pie you made yesterday."

"We think the old lead pipes in the barn poisoned the water. I'd been using that water to mix milk replacer. When Daniel got the delivery truck stuck in January, he broke a pipe, and I just shut the water off and didn't fix the broken pipe."

Jacob took a sip of his coffee and finished answering all of Rebecca's questions.

"I didn't realize he had turned off the water from the new barn and was using water from the old well. Those pipes are original to the barn and needed to be replaced years ago."

"Since we have other obligations to take care of this week in helping the Yoders, we'll have to wait until next week to figure out what repairs need to be completed before you bring any more livestock home."

Chapter 8

Samuel's Confusion

Ruth stood up to stretch as she rubbed her lower back that ached from sleeping in a chair for three nights. Levi left to get them a cup of coffee, and she was waiting patiently for the doctor to come in and talk to them. They'd been keeping Samuel sedated. When he was awake, he was combative and confused.

The doctors assured her that his shoulder would heal, but it was the look in his eyes that had her most concerned. She wasn't sure he remembered who she was, and he remembered nothing about the accident. The sheriff from Willow Springs stopped by to question him earlier in the day, but he couldn't remember anything about Saturday afternoon.

She had never seen this side of her son. He was loving and kind and never raised his voice, but the last couple days, he was short-tempered with everyone, including her.

Levi came back to the room at the exact same time the doctor stopped by on his rounds.

"Thank you for taking the time to talk to us this morning," Levi said. "We're very concerned about Samuel's personality changes. He's angry and violent, which is the complete opposite of how he normally is."

Dr. Hallman picked up his chart and started to read through some of the tests that they had run. "I ordered a series of tests that would tell me if the head trauma he suffered is anything to be concerned with. I believe he is suffering from retrograde amnesia. For some people, this type of amnesia affects the memories he had right before the accident.

"Most times, they'll lose the last three or four hours before the trauma. However, memories usually return in bits and pieces like a jigsaw puzzle over time. He may remember a face but not a name. There are even some instances when they forget someone that was an important part of their life, and almost always, there are changes in their personality. We need to do some further testing to see how severe his memory loss is, but for us to do that, we will need to stop sedating him."

"What about his anger?" Ruth asked.

"One of the effects of memory loss is a change in personality. Once he starts putting some of the pieces together, he should calm down and become more like his old self."

"We will need to keep him as calm as we can, and if anyone or anything upset him, I want to know."

Levi stood to see him out as Ruth brushed the hair off Samuel's forehead.

Once Levi returned, he sat down next to Ruth and took her hand to comfort her.

"It's been a long and trying few days, and I think we need a good night's sleep and a fresh change of clothes," he said.

"I think it's best we call Mr. Miller and have him come take us home. I need to check on the strawberries, and you need your own bed for a night. I'm going to call Jacob and see if he and Stella can come down and stay for the night so we can get some rest. We'll come back tomorrow afternoon after we have rested."

Ruth didn't argue, and even though she hated to leave Samuel, she needed a breath of fresh air and a few hours to rest in the comfort of her own bed.

Levi found a phone at the information desk and called the furniture shop.

Samuel had started to stir the minute he walked back in the room, and Ruth was trying to calm him down by talking in hushed whispers in his ear.

"Stop that? Where's Emma?"

Ruth looked up at Levi with questioning eyes.

"She's not here, son. I've already told you that you can see her when you go home."

Ruth moved away from him and let Levi come to his bedside.

"What am I doing here?" Samuel asked in a harsh tone as he looked up to his *datt*. "Is Emma okay?"

"You were in an accident a few days ago, and Emma is fine. It won't be long, and you'll be able to get up and move around," Levi stated.

Just at that moment, a nurse walked in to check his vitals and see if he was ready to drink something. After leaving a glass on his tray, she motioned for them to follow her to the door.

"I know this is disturbing to see your son like this, but please understand it is all part of the amnesia. His memories will start to return in bits and pieces, and until then, he is confused and hurting. I heard that you're planning on going home for the evening, which I think is best. He needs to be alone with his own thoughts for a little while, and once he starts putting the puzzle back together, he'll calm down."

Samuel turned his head to look at his parents. The look on his face was a blank stare, and Levi and Ruth were afraid to say anything to disrupt his concentration. He acted like he wanted to say something but didn't and instead turned to face the window.

As he looked out the window, he couldn't help but see the face of a woman he didn't know. The fear in her eyes and a loud noise kept haunting him. He didn't understand who she was and why he was in the hospital.

Everything was a blur. All he wanted to do was to talk to Emma. The last thing he could remember was talking to her when he went to deliver strawberries. He felt frustrated and couldn't understand why he was in the hospital and how he hurt his shoulder.

Who is this woman I keep seeing and why aren't my parents telling me what happened? he wondered.

Levi reached for Ruth's hand and pulled her out into the hallway.

"All we can do is pray that he will regain his memory, and he will return to us the same Samuel he has always been. We have to put our faith in *Gott* and be confident in what the doctors are telling us," he said.

Just then, they heard a loud crash and went back into the room to see the tray that sat in front of him had been turned over and thrown across the room. Ruth turned and ran for the nurse as Levi went in to try and calm him. It was all Levi could do to keep him still long enough until the nurses arrived to keep him from getting out of bed. He was determined to get out of bed and leave his room.

A team of nurses came in and asked Levi to take Ruth and leave the room until they got him calmed back down. They walked with their heads hung low to the end of the hall where a line of waiting room chairs were pushed up against the windows. The sun was bright and shining through the window. Ruth sat so the sun could warm her; she was cold and missed the peacefulness of home.

"I feel like I am in a nightmare, and I just need to wake up," she said.

"I know what you mean. I feel the same way."

After about twenty minutes, the nurse came and found them.

"I think we have him calmed down enough so you can go back in. We talked to the doctor, and he allowed us to remove his IV port since it's causing him so much anxiety. He seems more relaxed without all of those tubes and wires surrounding him," she stated.

Levi thanked her and started to stand. Ruth said she needed a few more minutes to herself before going back to his room. Levi looked into his *fraa*'s eyes and could see the strain she was under. Seeing Samuel like this was more than he could bear, and he could only imagine what it was doing to Ruth.

"Of course. You stay as long as you want. Jacob and Stella should be here anytime, and we can go home for the night. Things will look better in the morning," he said.

Ruth watched him walk away and turn to go back into her son's room. She closed her eyes and silently prayed that *Gott* would give Samuel his memory back and that she'd find a way to help him through this challenging period.

As soon as Levi came back into the room, Samuel turned his way and said he was hungry.

"Well, that's a good place to start. I'll go ask the nurse if you can have a bite to eat," Levi said.

Ruth stayed at the end of the hall for another thirty minutes and only got enough energy to get up once she saw a nurse carry a tray into Samuel's room. She hoped that meant he was asking for something to eat. Ruth stood outside the room as she waited for the nurse to leave the tray. She watched Levi add a straw to his covered drink and hold it close so Samuel could take a drink. He acted calm and more like himself.

When she walked into the room, he turned and looked at her. He kept looking at her as if he wanted to say something, but the words just wouldn't come. When he had had enough, he pushed the tray away and turned to the wall and closed his eyes.

Ruth went out into the hall just as Mr. Miller, Stella, and Jacob got off the elevator.

"We can't *denki* enough for coming for us and staying so we can go home to get some rest. Come sit with us and let us tell you what the doctors have said today," Levi said.

All five of them headed to the end of the hall and back to the chairs Ruth had just left a short time ago. Once they were all seated, Levi explained everything that Dr. Jennings had said. He described how Samuel's personality had changed, and the doctor felt that his head trauma was the cause of his memory loss. He felt he would start regaining some of his memory and start acting more like his old self again in a few days. Ruth explained how violent and combative he had become and how worried she was that he wouldn't regain all of his memory back.

"He's hot and cold. One minute he is calm, and the next minute he is throwing tantrums," Levi stated.

"I have to tell you that he keeps asking for Emma," Levi said.

Jacob looked at Stella as if to ask her if she knew what that was all about. Just then, Levi cleared his throat and, with a smile on his face, said, "I know that Samuel has been sweet on Emma for a couple years now, and with her birthday coming up, I'm sure he was going to start letting her know."

"That's news to us," Jacob said.

"I'm afraid if we can't get him to calm down, we may have to let Emma come talk to him. If that would be all right with you?" Levi asked.

"Well, isn't that something to think about, Samuel and Emma?"

In the back of his head, he couldn't help but think it might just be what they needed to keep Emma in Willow Springs.

Stella noticed the dark circles under Ruth's eyes and could see that she needed a break.

"I want to tell Samuel we're leaving and that you'll both be staying with him tonight."

As Ruth got up, everyone followed her back to the room. Samuel had fallen asleep and seemed to be resting so she didn't want to wake him. She had Jacob promise that he would send word if anything changed before they returned the following afternoon. Jacob asked Levi if he wanted them to stay in his room or just close by.

"I think he needs some space and time with his own thoughts, so if you could just stay close enough to be here if the doctors or nurses need us for anything, that would be great," Levi stated.

Mr. Miller reminded Jacob that he would return for them at four o'clock the following day and he would drop Levi and Ruth off at the front door and just wait for them without parking the van. They said their goodbyes, and Stella and Jacob went back to the chairs that overlooked the city. Stella pulled out her knitting, and Jacob pulled his pocket Bible out from his vest pocket.

As they both sat in the quiet of the hospital, Jacob couldn't help but remember the night he'd spent in the hospital sixteen years ago. Stella had gone into early labor the same night they had traveled to Sugarcreek to attend his *datt*'s funeral. An accident at the end of his *schwester*'s driveway had delayed him, and the scar on his face was a constant reminder of that night.

Chapter 9

A Mother's Plea

Daniel had just finished parking the delivery truck behind the Feed & Seed for the day when his father called.

"Son, how much longer do you think you'll be?"

"I'm just getting in my truck now to head home. Do you need something from town?"

"No, I don't need anything, but the Yoders could use some help if you're free. When I dropped them off at home, Levi said they had two carts of strawberries that needed to be delivered. They're shorthanded today, and there's no one to make Samuel's deliveries. One of the carts needs to be taken to the Haven Sandwich Shop and the other one to the Mercantile. I told Levi I'd call and see if you could help with those deliveries."

"Sure, I'll go over and see what I can do to help."

"When you get home, we need to talk about those letters from your mother. I noticed there was another one in the mail yesterday, and I'd like to talk to you about them."

"Dad, you know how I feel about her. I don't think there's anything you can say to make me change my mind."

"I know, son, but she's your mother and at least deserves a response from you."

"I'll think about it, and we can talk when I get home."

As he pulled out of the Feed & Seed, he started to mumble under his breath, "She may have given birth to me, but she hasn't been my mother for a long time. I don't even have any good memories of her. If you count going 'hungry and hiding in closets' mothering, then I'll just soon forget her altogether."

All the way to the Yoders, he had flashbacks of being taken from his grandmother when she got too sick to keep him. When she died, he was placed in his first foster home and never saw his mother again. Over the years, she'd sent a few letters but nothing consistent and nothing after she signed her rights away and let the Millers adopt him.

All of a sudden, six months ago, her letters got more frequent and always with the same request. She wanted to see him and wanted him to help her find Elizabeth. He had no desire to reconnect with her. His life was good in Willow Springs, and the only real parents he had were Mr. and Mrs. Miller.

When they adopted him, it was the happiest day of his life. His adoptive mother was kind, patient, and had introduced him to the Lord. His adoptive father was a strong and loyal Christian, and his faith was a real testament to the glory of God and his character. Daniel could only hope that he'd be half the man he was someday.

While stopped at a red light, he caught a glimpse of himself in the rearview mirror. His sandy blond hair reminded him that he wasn't a reflection of his adoptive parents, but that didn't matter to him at all. For the past ten years, he was Daniel Miller, and that was all he needed. No matter how hard he tried, he couldn't stop thinking about his biological mother begging for help. He could tell by her letters that she felt he was her only hope of finding Elizabeth.

How could he ever get past his anger and disappointment that he felt for his mother?

He couldn't shake the memories her letters stirred up—the sound of her cries as his father beat her, the darkness of someplace cold and wet, along with a strange noise he could never place. Would they ever stop haunting him? To make things worse, he still was having nightmares about a baby crying. Those dreams always left him with a feeling of dread that took him days to shake off.

He didn't know much about his biological father, and what he did know his grandmother had told him before she died. His father was an alcoholic and was forever stealing money from his mother that was meant for rent and groceries. Often, the results of his father's drinking left them homeless and living in his mother's car.

His mother worked as a waitress and often hid him in the car during her shifts and brought food out to him on her breaks. When she became pregnant and too far along to wait tables, the restaurant owner laid her off, promising she could come back after she had the baby and found a sitter. She never did make it back to work, and he ended up living with his grandmother. He never knew what happened to Elizabeth.

To block out the painful memories, he turned the radio on as he pulled onto Mystic Mill Road. As he got closer to Yoder's Strawberry Acres, he noticed there were still people picking berries and Emma and Katie were working the roadside stand. Levi was loading baskets into the back of a pickup truck when he pulled into the driveway.

"Daniel, it's so good to see you. Your father said he was going to call you. Are you available to make some deliveries today?"

"Yes, sir, just tell me where, and I'll be on my way."

"This wagon has two orders ready to go. Ten baskets go to Mr. Clamp at Haven Sandwich Shop and the other ten needs to go to the Mercantile. Do you want us to load them in your truck, or do you want to take the wagon?"

"It's such a nice afternoon, I think I'll deliver them in the wagon, if that is all right with you."

"Let me go get Izzy for you."

Daniel had spent two summers working on an Amish horse farm outside of Sugarcreek, Ohio, before moving to Pennsylvania, so he was comfortable driving a wagon. With the wagon loaded and Izzy all hooked up, he started on his way. As he came to the end of the driveway, he pulled up beside the stand and looked in Katie's and Emma's direction.

"Good afternoon, ladies."

Emma smiled as he tipped his hat to them both.

"Any word on Samuel today?" Daniel asked. "I was going to ask your father, but he was busy with a customer."

"*Datt* said he's confused and angry and doesn't remember much about Saturday. They're more concerned with his memory than his shoulder. The doctor said he'll need physical therapy on his shoulder once he comes home, and he's hopeful his memory will return in time," Katie stated.

"That's great news. I'll continue to pray for him. Well, I'd better get these berries delivered and get back before the sun goes down."

As soon as he pulled away, Katie busied herself at the end of the stand so she could watch him drive away. Secretly, she found him attractive and wished he was Amish.

He pulled the wagon away and turned back to wave at the girls when he saw Katie already looking his way. He immediately thought she had a sweet smile and wondered why he'd never noticed it before. It wasn't long, and his thoughts turned to Melinda. He was hoping she was working so he could say a quick hello and ask her about the volleyball tournament.

As he pulled behind the sandwich shop, the yellow crime scene tape was still in place at the Restaurant on the Corner's back parking lot. He still couldn't believe that someone was murdered and Samuel was shot while trying to save the young girl. The parking lot behind the Haven Sandwich Shop was full, so he pulled across the street to the area that had been reserved for horse and buggies. He tethered Izzy to the post and walked across the street to the sandwich shop. He knocked on the back door and waited for someone to answer.

"Daniel, what are you doing back here?"

"I'm helping Levi with Samuel's deliveries. I brought you ten baskets. I had to park the wagon across the street, so I'll carry them over as soon as you tell me where you want them."

"You can put them right here in the hallway, and when you're done, there's fresh pie in the case, if you're interested. I know how you have a liking for Mrs. Clamp's pies."

"Thanks, but I don't think I have time today. I still have to swing by the Mercantile before getting the cart back to Levi."

Mr. Clamp stood in the doorway just shaking his head as he looked across the parking lot and saw the yellow tape.

"We're still in shock about Samuel. We never have any trouble around here. Most of the time, the college kids are well behaved and don't cause any trouble. I hear that group wasn't even from

Willow Springs. They were just passing through on their way to Pittsburgh."

"I read in the *Willow Times* this morning that there hasn't been a murder in Willow Springs in twenty-five years," Daniel stated.

"Just a shame," Mr. Clamp said as he took the invoice out of Daniel's hand.

"Let me grab the cart, and I'll come out and help you carry the baskets in," he said.

The smells in the shop made his stomach growl, and he thought about taking Mr. Clamp up on his offer of a piece of pie. Just as he was about to go out the door, he heard someone call his name.

"Too good to come in the front door?" Melinda stated as she peeked her head around the kitchen door.

"No time today, but it sure does smell good. So, will I see you at the tournament on Friday?" he asked.

"I think my dad is coming around to the idea, but he hasn't given me a definite answer yet."

"Well, I'll keep my fingers crossed," he said.

"Come on, Daniel, quit flirting with the help, and let's get those berries carried in before Mrs. Clamp comes after us with her rolling pin."

Daniel winked at Melinda as they both chuckled at Mr. Clamp's comment.

It was almost dark by the time Daniel made it back to the Yoders. He took a few extra minutes to rub down Izzy and make sure she had fresh water and a scoop of grain before heading to his truck. Just as he turned the corner, he saw Katie and Emma carrying the cashbox and two extra baskets back to the barn. He waved as they started to walk his way. Katie walked up to him and asked if his mother would like the last two baskets of berries left over from that morning's picking.

"I'm sure she'd put them to good use. Let me pay you for them."

"Don't be silly. It's the least we can do after you made deliveries for us today," Katie said.

Emma had stopped to tie her sneaker and caught up with them just as he was taking the berries from Katie. He was glad he got a chance to say hello without her worrying if her dad would catch her talking to him.

He enjoyed how easy it was to talk to her, and if he ever found his sister, he'd want her to be just like Emma. She had a way of making him laugh, and he loved the way she found the good in everything and everybody. He could learn a great deal from her, especially when it came to how he felt about his mother.

He thanked Katie for the berries and climbed into his truck. He couldn't help but think how nice it had been driving the wagon. He missed working on the horse farm and his Amish friends in Sugarcreek. He did love his truck, but he had to admit the sound of the horse's hooves on the pavement and the slower pace had a soothing effect on him. The sun felt good and gave him plenty of time to think about the conversation his father wanted to have once he got home.

His mother had his supper on the table waiting for him as he came in the back door.

He put the baskets on the counter and pulled out his regular chair and said, "It smells wonderful, I'm starving."

"Your dad's already eaten and is in his office. He wants you to meet him there when you're finished," she said.

"I know he wants to talk to me about those letters from my mother. I'm not sure I want to do what she is asking or even if I want to see her again. It's been so long, and I've tried so hard to put all that behind me. If it wasn't for you and dad, who knows where I'd be."

"Son, your Christian duty is to forgive her and show her grace. She couldn't help what happened, and I'm sure she tried to protect you the best she could. It's been sixteen years, and I can only imagine she misses you and your sister."

"I guess it's not even about seeing her as much as it's about her wanting me to find Elizabeth. What if she doesn't want to be found? What can I do living here? She gave her away in Ohio. I'm not sure I want to stir this whole mess back up again."

He finished his supper and went to tell his father he'd be in after he got cleaned up.

He'd taken a shower, dressed, and was standing at his bedroom window, staring out at the library across the street. He loved living in Willow Springs. He enjoyed his job and didn't want his mother anywhere near the life he had made here and certainly didn't want to travel to Ohio to help her search for Elizabeth. The sun had set, and the streetlights were on as he watched a couple pushing a baby stroller and walking a dog. The sights made him remember how he prayed every night that his mother would come and get him and take him home. Those lonely years he'd spent in and out of foster homes still haunted him. All he ever wanted was a normal family.

His cell phone rang and startled him back to reality. He picked it up to see who it was, and when he didn't recognize the number, he laid it back down on the dresser and went downstairs to talk to his father. He found his father sitting at his desk typing on his laptop.

"Come in and sit down. Let me finish this email so we can talk."

It had only been a few seconds when his father closed his laptop, took his glasses off, and came to sit in the chair beside him.

Daniel stood up and walked to the window.

"I know you want me to answer those letters, but I just don't know if I want to do what she's asking of me. She wants me to help her find Elizabeth, and I just don't see how I can do that. She only has a few months left of her sentence, and I just don't understand why she won't wait.

"What can I do? In her letters, she said that all she has is a man's name and the street address of where she left my sister. She said she's sent many letters over the years and they've never been returned or answered. She isn't even sure the man lives at that address, but she's certain whoever lives there must know something of Elizabeth. She wants me to drive to Ohio and see if I can find the man she gave Elizabeth to. I can't help but think that if she hadn't made me run and hide in that ditch, she would've given me to some stranger too. I still have nightmares about that night, and the last thing I want to do is bring all that back up again."

"Son, all she wants you to do is drive to the address and ask a few questions. I can't see the harm in that. She's your mother, and no matter how you feel, I can't help but think she did what she felt was right at that moment. She knew enough to make you run and hide, and had Elizabeth been older she would have tried to hide her as well."

Daniel came and sat back down and put his head in his hands as his elbows rested on his knees. "In those nightmares, I always hear a baby crying, and I have to believe it was Elizabeth. I was hiding in the ditch and couldn't see what was going on, but I remember hearing my father scream at my mother to shut that baby up, or he was going to kill them both.

"I remember hearing another man's voice, but I never saw his face. After that, she came and got me out of the ditch, and we sat in the car until the police came. That was the last thing I remember before I was taken from her and dropped off at my grandmother's house."

"You know, if you do what your mother's asking, it may give you the closure you need, and the nightmares will stop. It might be a good thing if you found your sister. I'm sure she doesn't even know she has a brother."

Daniel stood up and walked back to the window. It was dark out, but he could still see the outline of the quaint little town he now called home.

"I'm so happy here," he said. "And I'm just afraid if I let my mother back into my world, things won't ever be the same again."

"Son, don't you think God has this? If you put your faith in Him, He won't lead you astray. I'd suggest you pray and ask Him to show you what He wants you to do. He'll tell you if you'll just look and listen. Until then, at least answer her letters and acknowledge you received them."

Daniel turned around to face his father and said, "I'll answer her tonight."

As he climbed the stairs to his bedroom, he couldn't help but stop on the steps and look at the family pictures his mother had hung on the wall. All showed a happy boy with two parents who took him in and gave him a family. He wondered if Elizabeth had a family and if she'd be excited to know she had a brother.

Once he returned to his bedroom, he sat down at his desk, turned on the desk lamp, and opened the top drawer to retrieve a pen and tablet.

> Mom,
>
> *I'm not sure I want to help you find Elizabeth. I know you want to see what happened to her and if she's willing to meet you, but what if she doesn't want to meet us? I can't help but think sixteen years is a long time, and it may be impossible for me to find her with so little information.*
>
> *I promise I will think about it and let you know what I decide.*
>
> *Daniel*

He put the letter in an envelope, sealed it, and wrote out the address to the Ohio Reformatory for Women in Marysville, Ohio. He was going to have to think long and hard about helping his mother, but for now, it had been a long day and morning would come early. He crawled into bed and shut off the light.

Chapter 10

My Emma

Emma spent the day helping Katie sell strawberries at the roadside stand, and was just about to head home when Levi called her name.

"Emma, can you come here for a minute? I need to talk to you about something."

She turned and headed in his direction and couldn't imagine what he needed to speak to her about. She followed him into the barn and stopped and waited for him to speak.

"Mr. Miller will be here shortly to pick us up and take us back to the hospital. I want you to come with us. I spoke to your *datt* when I called to check on Samuel, and he's given his permission for you to go."

Her heart skipped a beat knowing she was going to see Samuel. *Does* Datt *know how I feel about Samuel?* She thought. She couldn't imagine why she was being asked to go with them.

Levi knew she was full of questions but turned his attention to a stack of baskets that needed to be moved and said. "Mr. Miller will be here in thirty minutes. Can you be ready?"

"I'll hurry home and change my clothes. Can you pick me up there?" she asked.

As Levi turned to face her, he stopped as if he was trying to find the right words and said, "He's been asking for you, and we're hoping you'll be able to calm him down. He has been anxious and disoriented, and the only sense he's been making in days is his constant need to see you."

She didn't say a word and quickly turned to head home. She walked as fast as she could and, at times, almost running. Her mind was spinning and could hardly control her nerves at the thought of traveling away from the farm again. She didn't like the smell of the hospital, and the lights and traffic in Pittsburgh scared her; but she needed to see Samuel, and he was worth another trip to the city.

Once she got home, she was greeted at the door by Rebecca.

"Oh, good you're back. You can help us with supper before *Mamm* and *Datt* get home."

"Sorry, I can't. Mr. Yoder asked me to go to the hospital with them, and I need to get cleaned up and be ready to go in twenty minutes."

"Whatever for?" asked Rebecca.

Emma didn't want to go into a lengthy discussion, and she didn't want her *schwester* to know Samuel had been asking for her. Running up the stairs two at a time, she hollered over her shoulder, "I don't have time to explain."

Rebecca shook her head and turned to go back into the kitchen.

Upstairs in her room, Emma changed her dress and apron and unpinned her *kapp* to brush out her hair before she retwisted it in a bun and covered it up again. She glanced out the window to make sure Mr. Miller wasn't heading down the driveway before she turned to go downstairs to wait for him.

As she passed the kitchen, she heard Rebecca snapping at Anna to hurry up. She didn't understand why she had to be so bossy and was glad she was leaving and didn't have to put up with her older *schwester*.

Out on the porch, she sat in her favorite rocker that overlooked the garden on the far side of the house. From where she sat, she had a full view of the driveway and could see when they arrived. The garden needed to be weeded, and she made a mental note to get to it as soon as she returned from the hospital. She leaned back in the chair, closed her eyes, and said a silent prayer for Samuel and a safe return for her parents. She still couldn't believe Samuel had been asking for her and prayed that she could comfort him and see to his needs when she visited.

With her eyes still closed, she heard a car turn into the driveway and finished her prayer before she stood and walked to the front of the porch to wait for Mr. Miller to stop the van.

He pulled up to the steps and waved hello as she walked around the front of the van and climbed into the backseat beside Ruth. After she'd gotten her seatbelt on, he followed the circle driveway that led in front of the barn. As he drove by the barn, Matthew was coming out and walked over toward them. Mr. Miller slowed to a stop and rolled his window down. Levi leaned forward so he could see Matthew around Mr. Miller.

"We're heading back to the hospital to relieve your parents. Your *datt* gave us permission to take Emma back with us. I'm not sure if she'll be staying overnight or if she'll come back with your parents."

Matthew looked in the backseat to see Emma and then turned his attention back to Mr. Miller and asked, "What time do you think you'll have my parents back?"

"It depends on if I need to wait for Emma. If I just pick them up and leave, I should be back no later than seven thirty or eight. It's rush hour, so the traffic might slow me up a bit."

"Well, you'd better get going so you can get back. I'm sure my *datt* will be anxious to leave—he doesn't like hospitals much."

Levi waved back as Mr. Miller rolled up his window, and they headed down the driveway.

The drive to Pittsburgh seemed quicker that time, and Emma enjoyed watching the scenery go by. Before she knew it, she could see them approaching the city and knew it wouldn't be much longer before she could see Samuel.

She wondered what Mr. and Mrs. Yoder thought of him asking for her. She still couldn't believe her *datt* had allowed her to come. He'd been so distant and short with her lately; she was shocked. She wasn't going to question him and was just glad he did.

Mr. Miller pulled up to the hospital's front entrance and saw Jacob and Stella sitting on a bench near the front door.

"Well, I guess that answers our question. Emma must be staying."

Levi was the first to get out, and he opened the back door so Ruth and Emma could follow him.

Jacob and Stella saw them pull up and walked their way.

Jacob waved hello and was the first to speak.

"He's resting now. They gave him a sedative a short time ago. He's been restless and in a lot of pain today. They're trying a new pain medicine and something to help him sleep. Every time he fell asleep, he'd wake up thrashing and calling Emma's name."

"Did you speak to him today? Did he know who you were?" Ruth asked.

"We went in and sat with him a couple times, and he seemed to know who we were. He kept asking if Emma was all right, and no matter what we said, he was adamant we weren't telling him the truth. I half expect he thinks Emma was the girl that he saved from being shot," Jacob explained.

Emma looked at her *datt* as if to ask if it was all right to speak when she said, "He stopped and talked to me when he dropped off the strawberries on Saturday. Maybe I'm the last person he remembers talking to."

"That would make sense. The doctor said that the type of amnesia he has would block out the last few hours before a trauma. If you're the last person he remembers talking to, he might be confusing you with the girl he protected. Let's hope by seeing you, he'll calm down, and it will help him remember what happened," Levi said.

Jacob grabbed Stella's hand and said, "We're keeping Mr. Miller waiting. Let's get going so they can get upstairs before Samuel wakes up. Hopefully, with Emma here, and when he sees she's fine, he'll settle down."

With a stern voice, Jacob spoke to Emma, "You stay with the Yoders and don't go off anywhere by yourself. You understand?"

"Yes, sir," she said as she followed the Yoders into the hospital.

Stella laid her hand on Jacob's arm as she climbed into the van. "She'll be fine. There's no need to worry about her. Levi will keep an eye on our daughter."

As Mr. Miller pulled away, Jacob looked at Emma as she walked through the hospital doors. He couldn't believe sixteen years had gone by so quickly.

How am I ever going to deal with the chance she might leave our Amish community? He thought. *Is the secret we kept from her all these years going to change her?* His time was running out, and he knew it.

Once on the elevator, Emma's nerves started to get the best of her. She felt her mouth water and felt faint. The smell of the hospital and the small enclosed elevator made her claustrophobic. Just when she thought she would be ill, the doors opened, and she followed the Yoders down the hall that led to Samuel's room.

Ruth reached out and took her hand and patted it as she said, "I know you're nervous. The hospital has the same effect on me."

"I hope I can help. Do you really think he's confusing me with the girl from the parking lot?" she asked.

"I sure hope so because if he sees you and knows you're okay, maybe he will stop being so angry and believe we are telling him the truth about you."

Levi slowly opened his door and peeked in to see if he was sleeping. Just as he was about to open the door wider, he spotted Samuel's doctor standing at the nurse's station.

"Emma, why don't you go in and sit beside him in case he wakes up. Ruth and I are going to stay out here and talk to his doctor for a few minutes."

Emma hesitated and wasn't sure she wanted to go in alone.

"It's all right. We'll be right outside if he wakes up and needs us," Ruth said as she motioned for her to go inside.

She quietly stood at the end of his bed, looking at him. His shoulder was bandaged, and his left arm propped up on a pillow. His head was turned toward the window, and he looked peaceful as he slept. She had never seen anyone in a hospital bed before, and the sterile environment and the sounds of the heart monitor were all a bit overwhelming. Her heart ached to see him like this. He was a pillar of strength to her, and she didn't realize just how much she cared for him until she saw him lying there.

In an instant, her whole life seemed to flash in front of her. Even if she was only fifteen and shouldn't be thinking about getting married, at that moment, she felt destined that she would always take care of him. She quietly pulled a chair up on the right side of his bed between him and the door. His face was still turned toward the window as he slept. She had never touched him before, other than their fingers touching when he passed her a flower in the strawberry field, but at that moment, the urge to feel his hand in hers overtook her.

She gently turned his hand over so his palm was up, and she placed her hand on his. He had a small brush burn and bruise on his palm, and she tried not to touch it, in case it was sore and would wake him. She laid her hand inside of his and softly closed her hand around it.

His hand was firm, even though his body was weak. His hand reacted to her touch, and he tightened his grip on her hand. She was startled and looked up at him. He had turned his face from the window and was awake, looking at her.

A single tear fell down his cheek as he whispered, "My Emma."

They were the only words he said before he closed his eyes and went back to sleep. She heard Levi's voice outside the door and quickly removed her hand from his and sat back in her chair.

The door opened slowly, and Ruth walked in and asked, "I see he is still sleeping. Do you want to stay here, or do you want to come and sit in the chairs at the end of the hall with us until he wakes up?"

She wouldn't dream of leaving him then and told her that she was comfortable and would stay with him. She reassured her that she would come get them as soon as he woke up.

"The nurse said the sedative they gave him earlier wouldn't wear off for a couple more hours, and he would most likely sleep the rest of the day. The room is small, so we will be right down the hall if you need us."

Ruth joined Levi who was already settling into his favorite chair that overlooked the city. She stopped behind him and placed her hands on his shoulders.

"Do you think it's all right we leave Emma in there alone?" Levi reached up and grabbed his *fraa*'s hand.

"I don't see any harm in it, and if she's the only one he's asking for, then she's the best person to be at his side. I'm not surprised he's been asking for her. I've known for a couple years that he's been sweet on her. Emma just didn't know it, but she might know now when he wakes up and sees she's fine.

"I think Jacob was right about him confusing her with the girl from the parking lot. I hope by seeing her, he'll start remembering what actually happened. The doctor wants him to remember it on his own and said we shouldn't be the ones to tell him. He wants to be sure his memory comes back on his own without us explaining what happened."

"We didn't tell Emma. Should we tell her what the doctor said?"

Ruth didn't even let Levi answer before she turned and said, "You stay here. I'll go tell her."

Emma didn't hear Ruth come in until she felt her hand on her shoulder and looked up just in time to see her motion for her to come out in the hallway. Outside Samuel's room, Ruth explained to her what the doctor had said about letting him remember things all on his own. Emma nodded to let her know she understood and went back to sit with him at his bedside.

The sun had already set, and all the lights in the city were shining brightly. Emma walked over to the window to stretch her legs and had only been standing there a few minutes when Samuel started thrashing around in his bed and hollering "No!"

She ran to the opposite side of his bed, trying to comfort him, all the while trying to stay away from his bandaged shoulder. Before she knew what happened, his good arm pushed her so hard, it sent her backward falling on the heart monitor, which smashed up against the wall, making a loud noise. Within seconds, two nurses were picking her up off the floor, making sure she was all right.

As she stood up to compose herself, she said, "I think he was having a nightmare, and when I came over to calm him down, he pushed me and I fell backward. I hope I didn't break anything."

The nurse giggled and said, "These things are pretty sturdy, and once I get it back online, it will be fine. I guess we should have told you to watch out for his flying arm. He's been doing a lot of that the last couple days, and he's knocked more than one nurse down this week. He's pretty strong, and we've learned to stay clear of his good arm when he's sleeping."

Emma looked at him, and he was still sleeping; he didn't even realize what he'd done. She couldn't wait for him to wake up so she could tell him he'd knocked her to the ground. He'd get a good laugh out of that when he was better.

It didn't take long for the nurses to get things hooked back up and went back to their station in the hall. She was surprised that Levi and Ruth hadn't come in with all the commotion, but when she looked down the hallway, they weren't sitting in their regular chairs. She figured they'd gone for a walk or to get something to eat.

It was only a few minutes after the nurses left that Ruth came back carrying a sandwich and bottled water for her. She had a smile on her face as she said, "The nurses tell me you got within arm's reach of one of his nightmares."

"I sure did, and did they tell you I knocked over the heart monitor?"

Ruth covered her mouth and said, "On my! *Nee*."

"I can't wait for him to wake up and get better just so I can tease him about knocking me to the ground. He'll get a big kick out of that," Emma said.

"He sure will."

"Are you still all right sitting in here? If so, I'll go back and sit with Levi. He's a little restless and is having a hard time sitting still. I made him go for a walk with me, and that seemed to help, but he's had just about enough of the hospital.

"I forgot to tell you that when we talked to the doctor earlier, he said he was going to release Samuel tomorrow. He said he'd need a few months of physical therapy on his shoulder and wants us to see him next week in his office. He also said there was nothing he could do about his memory and that it would just take time, so there was no reason why he couldn't go home. He said his shoulder is doing great and didn't foresee any complications from the surgery. He said he was fortunate, but I say *Gott* was looking after him."

"*Gott* is good," Emma said as she sat down to open her sandwich.

"You come get me if you need a break," Ruth said as she turned to leave the room.

She didn't realize she was so hungry until the sandwich was in front of her. It had been a busy day at the strawberry stand, and she and Katie only had time to pop a few berries in their mouths between customers. Once she finished her sandwich and put the cap back on her water, she leaned back in the chair and looked over at Samuel. He seemed to be resting comfortably and hadn't stirred since he knocked her over.

The quietness of the room gave her time to think. She'd been so busy helping Katie, she hadn't had time to think again about the comment she overheard her *datt* say last weekend. When she thought of it, it confused and worried her.

What did he mean by saying my life would never be the same? She thought. *What is it that he needs to tell me that could be so terrible that my life would change forever?*

She didn't want her life to change. She loved her life, her Amish community, and wanted everything to stay the same. She was excited about her birthday and that she'd be able to attend the *singeons* with Katie. And if everything went as she thought it would, Samuel would ask to take her home, and they would start courting. It would still be a couple years before she would consider marrying, but she hoped that Samuel would be the one that would ask.

She stood up to throw her sandwich wrappers in the trash and walked back over to the window. As she looked out the window, she wondered what it would be like to live in the city—all those cars and noise. And by the looks of it, the houses were packed together like sardines. She couldn't imagine living anywhere else except in Willow Springs. She wondered if the people who lived in Pittsburgh knew what it was like to see the sun come up over a cornfield or the smell of apple blossoms in the spring.

Do they know that nature could wake them up with a rooster crowing and they didn't need an alarm clock? She thought. *Nothing was better than hearing birds chirp and the clip-clop of a buggy horse on a blacktop road. Would they enjoy it, or would they yearn to get back to the busyness of the city?* She hoped she'd never had to find out and couldn't wait to get back to the quietness of the farm.

Before she had a chance to think more about living in the city, she heard her name. She turned to see Samuel awake and looking her way.

"Emma, is that you?" he asked in a quiet whisper.

She went to his bedside and smiled down at him. "Yes, it's me."

"Thank *Gott*" was all he said as he closed his eyes once again.

She walked around the end of the bed and sat back down in her chair. She reached up and laid her hand over his, and he turned his palm over so he could fully grip her hand.

"I thought you'd been hurt and everyone was afraid to tell me."

"No, I wasn't hurt, I wasn't even with you. I was at home helping *Mamm* with supper."

"I keep having this nightmare where I hear a loud noise and I see a girl's face. Every time I see the face, it's your face I see. What happened? Why am I here, and how did I hurt my shoulder? I keep asking my parents, but they won't tell me. How come?"

"I wish I could tell you, but the doctor told your parents you need to remember on your own. What do you remember about Saturday?"

"What day is it?" he asked.

"It's Wednesday," she answered.

"I remember talking to you in the garden. I remember I asked if I could start writing to you and you said yes."

He stopped and turned toward the window as if he was trying to stop the memories from coming. When he turned back toward her, he said, "I remember seeing a man pointing a gun at a girl. Did he shoot me?"

"He did, and that's why you're here and why your shoulder is bandaged. You had surgery on Saturday night. The bullet hit an artery, and they had to go in and repair it."

"And the girl? Is she all right?"

"Wait, I pushed her out of the way and threw myself in front of the man pointing the gun. I saved her life."

He was trying to take in all the memories that were coming back and had to close his eyes to process them all.

Emma stood up and brushed the hair that had fallen in his face off to the side and leaned down and whispered in his ear, "It's going to be okay. You're safe, and so am I."

With that, he opened his eyes and looked at her. With a smile on his face, he said, "You still make me feel all warm and fuzzy, Emma Byler."

At that moment, he wished she was older than fifteen because he'd marry her tomorrow if he could. There was no one in the world that made him feel like she did, and he couldn't wait until he could tell her how much he cared.

Chapter 11

Daniel

It had been three weeks since Samuel had been released from the hospital, and she hadn't seen him once since they brought him home. Strawberry season had ended, and she wasn't needed to help Katie anymore. In his last letter he mentioned he was getting tired of therapy and was begging his *datt* to let him return to work. As Emma walked across the yard to the furniture shop she prayed that he'd be well enough to attend Sunday's *singeon*.

She stood on the steps of the furniture shop holding a tray with a pitcher of cold meadow tea and a plate of cookies still warm from the oven. Her stomach was turning with the thoughts of speaking to her *datt*. Any interaction with him lately always left her feeling confused and anxious. She balanced the tray on her hip and opened the door with her free hand. Once inside she was greeted by Kathryn, her *datt*'s bookkeeper.

"Emma, it's so good to see you. You haven't been out to visit with me for some time now. I've missed your smiling face."

"I know, I've been busy with the garden, and we've been canning peas."

She looked down the hallway that led to the workshop out back.

"Is my *datt* in here?" Emma asked.

"He sure is, you can go ahead and go on back. I think he is working on a pie safe near the back of the shop."

Emma slowly started down the hall and stopped at the door that led to the work area in the back of the building. The smell of wood and stain filled her nose and reminded her of a time she loved to come and help her *datt* in his shop. As she stood in the doorway, she scanned the building, looking to see where he was.

Jacob heard voices in the office and wondered who Kathryn was talking too. He started to walk to the office when he recognized Emma's voice and stayed put. From where he was standing, he saw her stop in the doorway and look around the workshop. She looked scared and uneasy and no longer looked like his little Emma. She was almost sixteen, and he couldn't prolong sitting down with her any longer.

What upset him the most was he knew he was the reason for the look on her face, and he hoped he hadn't waited too long to talk to her. It was time he put this whole mess to rest. He spent all those years protecting her, and it was time to do what his *schwester* had been begging him to do for months. She was still standing in the doorway when he came around a stack of wood.

"Is that for me?" he asked.

"*Mamm* told me to bring you a snack. She thought you might enjoy a break, and she knows how you like warm cookies."

She put the tray down on a small table that sat near the window and turned to leave.

"That was thoughtful of her. How about you join me?" he said as he pulled a chair out and sat down.

For a few moments, she just stood there and didn't move. For months, he'd barely spoken to her, and now he wanted her to join him. With her head hung low, she pulled the other chair out and sat down.

He had already started to pour tea into the glasses that were filled with ice. He handed her a glass and grabbed a cookie from the tray.

"Did you bake these?" he asked as he popped one in his mouth. "You make the best sugar cookies. They remind me of the cookies your *mommi* made when I was a boy."

Still in shock, all she could do was nod. If she was ever going to confront him about his strange behavior, now was the time. She took a sip of tea and set her glass down.

"I've wanted to ask you something. Would this be a good time?" she said with a shaky voice.

He could tell his anxiety had an effect on her. Just by her voice, he knew she was uncomfortable around him, and he didn't blame her.

How could I have let this happen? How could I let my own daughter be so uneasy around me? He thought.

"This is a perfect time, what is on your mind?"

At the last minute, she changed her mind and decided to ask about attending the youth *singeon* on Sunday.

"I wanted to know if it's still okay for me to go to the *singeon* on Sunday. You know it's my birthday. It's at the Yoders' this week, so I'll be close by. I could walk there with Rebecca and Anna, and I'd come home early." She barely took a breath after each sentence, and when she had run out of things to say, she just looked at him.

"Emma, we spoke of this already, and you'll be allowed to go on your birthday, just like your *schwesters* did."

All at once, she boldly asked. "Have I done something to upset you?" Trying not to look at him, she lowered her head and blinked away the tears forming in her eyes. She couldn't imagine what she'd done, but she had to find out.

For the longest time, he didn't say anything, and she feared she'd upset him even more.

"No, you've done nothing wrong," he said as he stood up. "I promise I'll explain everything soon, but for now, I have a pie safe to finish."

As he turned to go back to work, he said, "*Denki* for the snack and tell your mother to come out here. I'd like to speak to her."

Emma stood there for a good long time trying to figure out what had just happened. He did it again. The look on his face confused her, and he acted like he was mad at her.

She picked up the tray and headed for the side door to go back to the house. As she walked across the driveway, she saw Daniel's truck pull in. She turned around and waited for him to get closer.

She loved talking to him and tried to at least say hello whenever he came to visit Matthew. She still wasn't sure her *datt* approved of Daniel being Matthew's friend, but right now, she didn't care who saw her talk to him.

Daniel slowed the truck and rolled down his window when he noticed she had turned to wait for him to go past.

"Beautiful day, don't ya think?" he asked as he pulled up beside her.

"It sure is, and the sun feels good and warm today. I thought you might like a few cookies before I take these back to the house."

He reached for a cookie and asked, "Is your brother here?"

"I think he's in the barn. He's been busy replacing pipes."

"Have you heard any more about Samuel?" he asked.

She moved closer to the truck window and said, "He came home a few weeks ago, and according to Katie, he's giving his therapist a hard time, so he must be feeling better. I overheard Mr. Yoder tell my *datt* that the police want to talk to him, but the bishop is refusing. He feels it wouldn't be in the best interest of the community."

"I can see how the bishop wouldn't like it if he made a statement or pressed charges. I would think they'd want him to be a witness in that boy's trial. I bet the bishop won't let that happen," Daniel stated. "How are the strawberries coming? I didn't see anybody at the stand when I drove past just now."

"The season's over, and I haven't had to help Katie at the stand or pick berries all week. Berry picking usually ends right around my birthday," she mentioned as she looked up to make sure her *datt* wasn't watching her speak to Daniel too long. She hoped he was still busy in the back of the shop.

"So, when is your big day?" Daniel asked.

"July seventeenth. This Sunday, I'll be sixteen. Well, I had better get back in the house before I'm missed. Go ahead and go out to the barn. I am sure you'll find Matthew there."

As he pulled away, he couldn't help thinking that Elizabeth would be about sixteen right now. He still couldn't help thinking she may not want to be found and reunited with him and his mother. He was hoping Matthew could help him figure out what he should do.

He parked his truck and started looking for his friend. When he found him, he was in the back of the barn kneeling, hammering on an old pipe. Matthew stood when he heard someone come in.

"Hello," he said as he brushed the dirt off his knees with the back of his hat. "What has you out here this time of day?" he asked.

"I was done early with my deliveries and thought I'd come out and talk to you before I headed home."

"Sure, what's on your mind?"

"Just how much time can you spare?" Daniel asked.

"Well by the looks of how I'm struggling with this pipe, I need a break and can take as long as you need." He turned a bucket over and sat on it.

Daniel followed suit and found another bucket and sat across from him. He picked up a piece of straw from the barn floor and started to twist it in his fingers.

"There are some things from my past I've never talked about but need to sort through."

"I'm not sure I'll have any answers, but I can certainly lend an ear," Matthew said.

"I'm not even sure where to start."

Matthew reached for his bottle of water as he said, "The beginning is always a good place."

"Okay…here goes," Daniel said. "You already know I was adopted by the Millers when I was ten, but I've never told you how I ended up in foster care."

Daniel sighed and started to roll the piece of straw between his fingers, trying to will himself into reciting a part of his life he wished he didn't remember.

"My biological father was a drunk, and my mother had a hard time keeping the rent paid." Again, he played with the straw waiting for the words to come.

"He pushed her around a good bit. There were many nights she would lock me in a closet at the bottom of the stairs. I was told not to open the door or make a sound until she let me out. As I look back on it, I know she was trying to keep me safe.

"As it turned out, in one of his fits of rage, she had had enough and killed him. She was sent to prison, and I was sent to live with my grandmother. I'd only been with my grandmother a year before she died. At that point, I became a ward of the state and sent to a foster home." He looked up just as Matthew started to say something.

"Wait, that's not the whole story—there's more. My mother is serving a fifteen-to-twenty-year prison term and is scheduled to be released early within the next few months. I have a younger sister named Elizabeth that she gave away and now wants me to find."

"I take it you don't want to find her?" Matthew asked.

"It's not that I don't want to find her—it's just that I have a sinking feeling that she may not even know she has a mother who's in prison or has an older brother. She was only a couple weeks old and won't even remember us even if she knew we existed. Can you imagine how traumatic that might be to her?"

"Wait a second. What do you mean she gave your sister away?"

Daniel dropped the straw and reached for another piece off the floor as he said, "I really don't have the whole story other than she gave her to someone before the police came and arrested her. As far as I know, the police didn't know she had any other children. All she has is an address to a farm in Ohio and wants me to go and ask some questions."

"Ohio? Where in Ohio?" Matthew asked.

"Sugarcreek. I have the address written down at home," Daniel said.

Hearing Daniel mention Sugarcreek, he immediately thought of Sarah. She was staying in Sugarcreek taking care of her *schwester*'s *kinner*.

"What does your mother want you to do if you find her?"

"All she wants to know is how she is and what became of her. I think she wants to see her after she gets out," Daniel said.

"I still can't believe she would just give her away, and I am struggling to forgive her," Daniel said as he stood to walk over to the open barn door.

"I have a week's vacation coming up, and I'm thinking about driving to Holmes County to ask some questions."

Matthew followed him and stood next to him as they both walked out and leaned on the fence that overlooked the alpaca's pasture. Matthew wasn't sure how he could help his friend deal with forgiving his mother, but he could lend a hand if Daniel needed it.

"I have all my fields plowed and planted and am almost finished replacing all the old pipes in the barn. I could use a change of scenery. Would you like some company?"

Daniel smiled at Matthew's offer. "That would be great. I start my vacation on Saturday after my last delivery. Would that be too soon for you to leave with me?" He asked.

"Let me clear things with my *datt*, but I'm sure that would work out just fine."

Jacob finished putting the last coat of walnut stain on the pie safe and was washing his hands in the sink under the window that overlooked the barn. He saw Matthew and Daniel standing near the fence, deep in conversation. He still wasn't comfortable with the friendship his son had with the English boy, but so far, Matthew gave him no indication that Daniel was encouraging him to leave his Amish community.

As he watched his son, his eyes caught a glimpse of Emma hanging clothes on the line. Sitting right beside her was that silly dog Someday. They still had no idea where the dog came from; he just showed up one day. She had instantly fallen in love with it, and he didn't have the heart to make her find it a new home.

He pulled his *schwester*'s latest letter from his pocket and read it one more time.

> Dear Jacob,
>
>   *I know you've been struggling for a very long time with what happened all those years ago, but it's time we deal with the decisions and promises we made. Marie Cooper continues to write asking for any information we have about her daughter. I've not replied to any of her*

letters, but she's due to be released from prison soon, and I'm sure she'll show up on my doorstep at some point. Before that happens, we must tell Emma. Walter made a promise to her that we must keep.

Anna Mae

He couldn't help but feel a sense of dread fall over him. His *schwester* has been through so much since Walter died. He just hated the turmoil she was in, anticipating the visit she was sure to get from Marie Cooper. If only Walter were still alive.

He died years ago from a massive heart attack, which left her alone to raise seven *kinner* by herself. Anna Mae was older than Jacob, and most of her *kinner* were now adults and out on their own. Her oldest son, Martin, had taken over the farm when Walter died. Anna Mae lived in the small *doddi haus* next to the main house that Martin and his family now lived in.

Jacob was raised in Holmes County, Ohio, and had not been back to visit his family since the death of his *datt*. That was the reason he was in Ohio sixteen years ago. He knew this day would come. Walter made a promise that he needed to keep, no matter how hard it would be. Just as he tucked the letter back into his shirt pocket, Stella walked into the workshop.

"Emma told me you wanted to see me. Sorry it took me so long, I wanted to finish getting supper in the oven before I left the kitchen."

Jacob rubbed the scar on his chin and said, "Anna Mae has written me another letter, and I just can't put her off any longer. The promise I made to Walter has to be kept, and it's my responsibility to see that it's carried out. Marie Cooper is due to be released from prison soon and will most likely pay a visit to Sugarcreek. The only address she has is that of Anna Mae's, so that's the first place I'm sure she'll go. I cannot let her deal with this herself. It was a decision the four of us made, and I must see that it's carried out."

Stella stood beside him and took his hands in hers. His hands were rough from years of working with wood, but they were still as strong and steady as they had always been.

Jacob pulled Stella into his arms and kissed her temple as he said, "Emma's birthday is on Sunday, and I'd like to talk to her after church. I don't know how she'll handle it, but I'll be praying that *Gott* will give me the words and that Emma will not hold any hard feelings toward us."

With that, he held out his hand, sat in the chair near the window, and pulled Stella to sit on his lap. They sat for a long time just enjoying the breeze coming in through the window.

Stella leaned down to get a better view out the window when she said, "I wonder what Matthew and Daniel are talking so hard about. Daniel looks upset. I've always liked him. There's something so familiar about him, but I've never quite been able to place what it is. He has a kind, caring heart and is easy to talk to."

"Mr. Miller helped us a lot when Samuel was in the hospital, and if he's half the man his father is, I'm sure he's a good friend to Matthew."

"Then it's settled. We'll talk with Emma on Sunday. Do you think we should include the rest of the *kinner*?"

Jacob had thought for a minute before he replied.

"Not now. Let Emma absorb all we have to tell her, and then we can tell the other *kinner* after Emma has had time to ask her questions."

"Supper will be ready shortly. Are you almost finished for the day?"

Jacob stood beside her and placed his hand on the small of her back directing her as they left the workshop together.

"Let me go check with Kathryn and make sure she doesn't need anything before I quit for the day."

Stella opened the workshop door just as Daniel and Matthew were walking toward his truck. Daniel stopped and turned once he heard the door open.

Daniel tipped his hat and said hello as he turned and walked toward her.

"Hello, Daniel, it's so good to see you. Did you and Matthew have a nice visit?"

"We did. He's a good friend, and he helped me sort some things out. Well, I'd best be going. My mother will be wondering what's taking me so long to get home. She likes to have supper waiting on the table for Dad and me as soon as we walk in the door."

Daniel climbed into his truck, and Matthew said he'd see him on Saturday and would be ready to go when he got here.

Stella looked at her son as Daniel pulled his truck away from the barn and asked, "Where are you going?"

"Daniel's going on vacation to Ohio for a few days and has asked me to go with him. I told him I needed to clear it with *Datt* first, but I can't see any reason it wouldn't be okay. My fields are all planted, and the pipes all fixed. It might be a good time to take a few days off.

"Where is he? I'd like to talk to him now."

"He was headed to talk to Kathryn and then he was closing up the shop for the day. He should be coming in for supper shortly."

Just as Matthew turned to head to the shop, Jacob turned the corner and came upon them both.

"There you are. I was just coming to talk to you," Matthew said.

"I'm right here, what's on your mind? Let's go take a look at how you're coming with those pipes, and you can talk to me then."

"Don't forget supper is almost ready and will be on the table when you're done in the barn," Stella hollered over her shoulder.

Chapter 12

A Trip to Sugarcreek

It was a beautiful Saturday, and Emma had spent most of the morning outside in the garden. She'd picked green beans and weeded the garden until it looked neat and tidy. It was nearly noon, and she had walked to the end of the driveway, pulling a wagon full of bright red geraniums and impatiens behind her. She loved planting flowers and was in charge of keeping the garden around her *datt*'s furniture shop sign looking pretty. Rebecca and Anna had brought the flowers home from the market yesterday to surprise her for her birthday.

As she walked down the driveway, she smiled at the thought of church being held at the Yoders' the following day and at seeing Samuel. It had been weeks since she'd spent the night with him at the hospital, and she missed him. She had received a letter from him on the last two Wednesdays and had read them over and over again.

He told her all about his physical therapy and how excited he was to see her at the *singeon* the following night. He had mentioned that the bishop had been by to talk to him about the shooting and had reminded him that the *Ordnung* forbade him to press charges against the young man who shot him. She hoped to see him that afternoon when she delivered the bread her mother was making, to help Ruth with the lunch meal after Sunday service.

Just as she sat down on the ground and started to pull out the wilted pansies she had planted earlier that spring, Daniel turned into the driveway and pulled his truck up beside her. He put the truck in Park and came around the other side of the truck to talk to her.

"You always keep these flowers looking nice," he said as he pulled the wagon closer and helped her take the pots of flowers out and place them on the ground in front of her.

As she reached for her small shovel, she said, "My *mamm* enjoys the gardens around the house looking neat and tidy, and I'm glad it's my job to work on them."

"Well, you do a good job," he said.

"So, I hear Matthew's taking a trip with you. What kind of trouble are the two of you going to get in? I hope it's something fun. He has been moping around here for months, and I haven't seen him smile in a very long time."

"I wish we had something fun planned, but he's just riding along with me while I go on a wild goose chase to Ohio looking for my sister," he said as he picked up the pile of weeds and put them in the wagon for her.

"Your sister? I didn't know you had a sister. I thought you were adopted and an only child," she said as she looked up at him, waiting for a response.

Daniel sat down on the grass beside her and started handing her the pots of geraniums so she could plant them in the newly dug holes.

"I was adopted by Mr. and Mrs. Miller, but I'd spent lots of years in foster care before I came to live with them. My sister is five years younger than me and was just a newborn when my mother gave her up. I really don't even remember her, and she was only a couple weeks old when my mom got sent to prison. She's due to be released from prison soon and intends to reconnect with us once she gets out."

"I bet your mother misses her, and if she has spent so many years not knowing what happened to her, I can see why she is anxious to find her. Do you know where you might start looking for her?"

"All I have is an address, but it's a place to start."

"Where in Ohio are you going?" she asked.

"Sugarcreek is the address I have. I'm originally from Ohio— that's where I was born and where my mom and I lived. Mom worked at a restaurant in Sugarcreek, and that's where I used to live with my grandmother before she got sick and died. I just want to forget that part of my life.

"Don't get me wrong, I have some great memories of going to high school there, and I worked on a great horse farm during the summers. It's also where my adoptive parents lived when I got placed when them. So, it's not all bad—just the part when my mother went to prison, and I spent so much time in foster homes."

Emma wanted to ask why his mother was in prison but figured if he wanted to share that with her, he would have. So far, he had eluded to the reason why.

"I'm not trying to side with your mother, and I can see you're not too excited about doing what she is asking you to do, but I think your sister deserves to know she has a brother. What if she's been in and out of foster care like you were and still doesn't have a family? How old would she be now?"

"She'd be about sixteen. I hadn't given any thought to the chance she might not have a family."

He was quiet for a few minutes while he kept handing Emma the pots of flowers.

"I can't stomach the thought of her spending her life in foster care. What if she's been wondering what happened to her real parents all these years? Thank you, Emma, I needed to see the other side of this. I've been spending so much time thinking about how I didn't want to drive to Ohio looking for someone who might not want to be found. I never gave thought that she might be looking for us. I hope when I do find her, she is as easy to talk to as you are."

With a new sense of purpose, he stood up and brushed off his pants as he climbed back in his truck.

"I'd better go get Matthew and be on my way. It's time I found my sister."

Emma smiled and went back to working on planting her flowers. She hoped Daniel found his sister and thought that any girl would be proud to call him her brother.

Matthew was in his room packing when he heard Daniel's truck come down the driveway. His *datt* wasn't too happy he was going to Ohio with him, but since he hadn't taken his baptism yet and technically was still in his *rumshpringa*, he couldn't do anything but shake his head and tell him to be careful. Matthew didn't say why they were going to Ohio; he didn't feel it was his place to explain that Daniel's mother had given his sister away to a stranger. If they found his sister, he would explain. He finished packing his bag and started down the steps as he heard Daniel knock on the front door.

Jacob was in the kitchen and hollered for him to come in. Jacob was sitting at the table reading the paper and drinking a glass of meadow tea as both of the boys came in the room.

"Take a seat and have some dinner before you start your trip. Matthew tells me you're headed to Sugarcreek. I was raised there and still have a sister who lives on the family farm. I hope you don't mind, but I've asked Matthew to stop by and check on his aunt while you're there. He has her address, and I hope you can find some time to stop by and say hello while you're in the area."

"That will be fine. I'll make sure he sees her," Daniel said.

The three men sat for a good while as they discussed the path they would take to Sugarcreek and the progress Matthew had made in repairing the barn.

Stella placed a platter of meatloaf on the table just as the twins and Emma came in from outside.

"I was just about to call you girls in for dinner. Go wash up, and we will eat before the boys head off on their trip," Stella said.

Once everyone was seated, Jacob bowed his head and said a silent prayer. Emma prayed that Daniel would find his sister and that she'd be excited to know she had family that loved her enough to look for her. Matthew's prayer included a desire to see Sarah while he was in Sugarcreek.

Jacob cleared his throat, indicating prayer time had ended and reached for the dish of pickled eggs in front of him. Looking at Daniel, he asked, "Where will you be staying once you get to Sugarcreek?"

Daniel put a scoop of mashed potatoes on his plate as they were passed around the table and answered, "I worked at a horse farm for a couple summers when we lived there, and the man who owns the farm has a loft in the barn for his farm hands. He told me that I was always welcome to stay there whenever I felt like a visit.

"He lost his wife last year, and I've meant to go visit with him. I'm pretty sure he'll be happy to see me and offer us a place to stay. If he doesn't have room, there's a hotel in Sugarcreek we can stay at."

"Don't waste your money on a hotel. Matthew's Aunt Anna Mae will be happy to put you up during your stay if your friend doesn't have room," Jacob said.

After everyone had finished their dinner, Jacob pushed himself away from the table and stood up and said, "I'd better be getting back to work. It's only a couple hours' drive to Sugarcreek, so you boys better get on the road. When do you think you'll be back?"

"I only have a weeks' vacation and have to be back to work a week from Monday. It shouldn't take me too long to do the business I need to take care of. And of course, making sure Matthew gets to his aunt's house. I'm planning to stay all week if Matthew is okay with that," Daniel said as he looked at his friend.

Matthew smiled and said, "You're in the driver's seat. I'm only along for the ride."

Stella stood up and started to walk into the other room as she said, "I have something I want you to take to your aunt. I just finished knitting a new lap blanket that she'll enjoy come winter."

Rebecca stood up and followed her mother as she asked, "Does Aunt Anna Mae knit or crochet? I could send her some skeins of my alpaca yarn that I just finished spinning."

"If I remember correctly, she likes to crochet, and I bet she'd love some of your yarn," Stella said.

Emma started to clear the table as Anna filled the sink with water to wash up the dinner dishes. Emma enjoyed seeing the smile on Matthew's face; he seemed to be excited to be going with Daniel. Ever since Sarah left last year, he hadn't smiled much. She didn't think anyone knew how he felt about Sarah, and she only knew because she saw them exchange a note right before she left last year. He'd been spending all his time in the fields or in the barn and hadn't gone to a youth *singeon* in over a year. For Emma, it would be good for him, to get away, if only for a week.

Stella placed the lap blanket and yarn in a canvas bag and handed it to Matthew as she said, "You be sure you find time to go visit with your aunt and your cousins while you are in Sugarcreek. Many of your cousins you've never even met."

Matthew took the bag, picked up his small suitcase, and followed Daniel out the front door and down the steps to his truck that was parked by the barn. They both climbed in and slowly backed up and headed down the driveway.

"Are you ready for our fact-finding mission?" Daniel asked.

"I am, and I have a mission of my own that I haven't told you about yet," Matthew said.

"I'm all ears. You have two hours to fill me in."

Emma let the twins finish the dishes as she grabbed the broom to go sweep off the front porch. It had rained the previous night and blew some of the fern leaves onto the porch from the plants that hung between the pillars of the porch. The porch was her favorite part of the large farmhouse. She could curl up in one of her *datt*'s chairs and rock for hours. Just as she finished sweeping off the last step, she heard the sound of her best friend Katie's voice as she walked up the driveway.

"Hello there," Katie hollered.

"Katie, it's so good to see you. What a lovely surprise."

"I was going to walk to your house this afternoon. *Mamm* wanted me to deliver the bread she made this morning," Emma said. Emma had hoped to get a chance to see Samuel and was a bit disappointed that her friend had surprised her with a visit before she got a chance to deliver bread to her *mamm*.

"My *mamm* wanted me to bring back a dish she borrowed, and since I'd finished my chores for the day, she said I could come and visit with you."

"We just finished dinner, and I have to take the clothes off the line and put them away before my chores are done. Can you stay that long?"

"Could you use two extra hands? If I help, you'll get done even faster, and then maybe we can go wading in the creek. We could ask Anna and Rebecca if they want to come along," Katie said as she set the dish on the step and followed Emma to the clothesline.

"That would be wonderful. I haven't gone wading yet this year. I doubt the girls will want to go. They just mentioned at dinner that they were washing alpaca fiber this afternoon, and that usually keeps them pretty busy for hours," she said as she started to take the clothes down from the line.

Katie walked to the other end of the clothesline and started to unfasten the line of blue dresses and trousers as she asked, "Are you getting excited about the *singeon* tomorrow night? Is your *datt* really going to let you go?"

"He told me the other day he wanted to talk to me after church tomorrow, and right now, that's all I can think about. I'm not sure what it's all about, but he seems so serious. I know I'm allowed to go, and Rebecca and Anna said I could walk with them. I think both of them have plans to be taken home, but with whom, I don't know."

"Good thing it's at your house, and I can just walk back through the field. I don't think *Datt* would want me to walk on the road at night, but since the corn is barely knee high, I can walk through the field. It's been weird around here the last couple days. For months, he's been moody and anxious about me going anywhere, but the last few days, I sense he's come to terms with whatever's been bothering him."

"Speaking of moody, Samuel's been impossible lately. I know his shoulder hurts and he hates physical therapy, but he's no fun to be around anymore. He cornered me outside this morning when he heard *Mamm* tell me to bring the dish back. He wanted me to find out if you were going tomorrow night."

Emma had her back to her friend and couldn't help but smile at the thought of Samuel asking about her. "You can tell him, as far as I know, I am."

Emma finished folding the last of her *schwester*'s aprons and picked up the basket to carry inside. "Let me go put these clothes away, and we can go down to the creek."

"I'll take the dish inside and come back on the porch and wait for you to get done," Katie said.

"Perfect, I won't be long."

Katie set the dish on the counter and said hello to Rebecca and Anna. They were just finishing up the dishes and were headed out to the alpaca barn.

"Emma and I are going wading in the creek. Do you want to come?"

"We need to get the alpaca fiber all washed and hung on the drying racks to dry. We better not take time out to go for a walk until our chores are done. *Denki* for asking, and maybe we can go the next time you come over," Anna said as she reached to hang the towel on the hook by the sink.

Katie followed the twins back outside and sat down in one of the rockers near the front door. As she sat, she couldn't help but think about the short conversation she just had with Daniel and Matthew on her walk over to Emma's.

Daniel had pulled up beside her on the road. He was going in the opposite direction but wanted to make sure she didn't need a ride somewhere. When he found out she was just going to Emma's, he laughed and said he thought she could handle the walk since she was almost there.

Katie wasn't sure what it was about Daniel, but she found herself looking forward to seeing him more and more. He wasn't Amish, and she had no desire to leave her community. She just needed to push those silly thoughts of Daniel Miller out of her head.

Daniel smiled as he pulled back on the road after checking to see if Katie needed a ride.

"I never took notice of her before, but she has the prettiest smile—you just can't help smiling back at her," Daniel said as he slowed down and passed the buggy in front of him.

"I thought you were sweet on Melinda from the sandwich shop," Matthew asked.

"I thought so too. But there is something sweeter about Katie Yoder."

Matthew laughed and said, "Not sure that can go anywhere since you're not Amish."

"Enough about my loveless life. Tell me about this mission you're on," Daniel said.

"I guess I should tell you why it was so easy for you to talk me into going to Sugarcreek." Matthew said. "I thought it was because you were my friend and wanted to help me find my sister." "It's that too, but I have to admit I have someone I want to look for as well."

Daniel rolled up his window so he wouldn't miss any of what Matthew was saying. "Go on, I'm listening."

"My family doesn't know, but I'd been courting Sarah Mast for the last couple years, and I was just about to ask her to marry me when her *datt* sent her to live in Sugarcreek. Her brother-in-law needed help taking care of her niece and nephew after her *schwester* died. That was a year ago, and I've not heard a word from her since. She promised she'd write to me, but I've heard nothing. She never told her family she was seeing anyone. She hadn't wanted to tell anyone at the time because they'd been so upset about her *schwester*.

"I just have to find out why she hasn't written or tried to get in touch with me. I'm afraid she's met someone in Sugarcreek and doesn't know how to tell me. I want to see her and find out for sure."

"Do you know who her brother-in-law is or where he lives?"

"I don't even know his name. I'm hoping when we go see my aunt, she might know of a widower with small children. I thought that might be a good place to start."

"We'll find her. I know a few Amish families in Sugarcreek, so we can ask around when we get there."

"Tell me about your work on the horse farm," Matthew asked.

"My father knew a few of the Amish families in the area, and I'd been begging him to learn how to ride a horse when he met Nathan Bouteright. Nathan was looking for stable boys, and my dad thought it would make a good summer job for me. In exchange for cleaning out the stalls, Nathan taught me how to ride and care for horses.

"I worked for him during the summers before we moved to Willow Springs. His farm was only a couple miles from where we lived so I could ride my bike there, but I ended up staying in the loft all summer. I'm looking forward to seeing him. He lost his wife last year, and I want to see how he's doing. I heard he took it pretty hard, and I've meant to go see him."

"Do you know how he lost his wife?"

"I'm really not sure. I guess I never heard how she died. I know they had a couple of kids."

Matthew couldn't help but think that it might be possible that Nathan could be Sarah's brother-in-law. "How old is he?" Matthew asked.

Daniel reached for his water bottle and said, "I think he is in his forties."

Matthew started to do the math in his head and figured Sarah's *schwester* was only a few years older than him. They all had gone to school together, and her *schwester* moved to Sugarcreek to teach as soon as she graduated. She couldn't have been more than twenty-five when she died. He figured that was too young to be married to a forty-year-old.

"Are you sure Nathan won't mind us staying in the loft?" Matthew asked.

"I'm sure he'll enjoy the company," Daniel said.

The rest of their ride was quiet. Matthew was lost in his thoughts about finding Sarah and Daniel was trying to figure out what he'd say to his sister if he found her.

It was almost three o'clock when they first saw the signs to Sugarcreek. Daniel had to admit he was excited to be back in his hometown.

"It won't be long now. Nathan's farm is only a few miles outside of town."

Matthew didn't get the opportunity to travel outside of Willow Springs much and was enjoying taking in the scenery. The landscape wasn't that much different than at home, and once they turned down the road that led to the Bouteright Farm, things started to look a lot like Willow Springs. White clapboard houses; dairy barns; lush, open green pastures; Jersey cows starting to make their way to the barns for evening milking; and *kinner* playing under the shade of big maple trees—looked pretty much like home. If he hadn't known he traveled two hours to get there, he'd still think he was in Pennsylvania.

When Daniel started to slow down, he turned to Matthew and said, "We're here. This lane leads back to Nathan's farm right over that ridge. He owns all of this pasture, and if you look over toward the woods line, you can see some of his horses grazing in the north field."

Matthew looked the way Daniel had pointed and could see at least ten horses enjoying the shade of the big trees near the fence line.

"That's an amazing sight! How many stable hands does he have working for him?"

"When I worked for him, he had at least four or five working every day. Since I only worked the summers, I didn't get to do much other than clean stalls and stack feed. His regular stable hands got to work with the horses on a daily basis.

"He takes in about twenty to thirty retired racehorses each year and trains them to pull buggies. He sells them and has them delivered to Amish communities throughout Pennsylvania and Ohio. I'm sure some of his horses have even made it to Willow Springs."

As they came up over the ridge, Matthew was in awe of the horse farm that was spread out in front of him. As they got closer, Daniel pulled his truck to a stop. Matthew noticed the farmhouse sat directly in the center of the farm. To the left of the main house was the *doddi haus*, with two rockers sitting on the front porch. In the middle and set back from the two houses were three huge horse stables. Around the back of the stables were paddocks surrounded by split rail fences. The garden to the left of the small house was lined with sunflowers that were just starting to bloom, and from where he was, it looked like a woman and two small *kinner* were working in it.

On the porch of the main house, an older woman sat with a yellow Lab at her feet. For as far as Matthew could see, there were horses and stable hands working every corner of the farm. One was working with a horse pulling a buggy around the perimeter of the horse stable, another was pushing a wheelbarrow around to the back of the first barn, and an older man was walking a horse inside one of the paddocks along the back of the stable. As far as he could tell, this was a large operation and he'd love to spend all his time getting to know how the farm operated.

As Daniel opened his door, he hollered toward the man walking the horse, "Nathan Bouteright, that's a mighty fine horse you have there."

Nathan didn't need to turn around to see who just pulled into the farm. He knew just by his voice that it was his favorite stable boy, Daniel Miller.

"Horse manure gets into your blood, doesn't it? Are you back looking to get thrown in the manure pile again?" Nathan unhitched the lead from the horse he was working with and let him free inside the closed paddock.

Daniel started to laugh at the memory of losing a bet he'd made with another stable hand, resulting in taking a dip in a fresh manure pile.

"That's one bet I wouldn't take kindly to repeating," Daniel said.

Nathan crawled over the fence and was standing next to Daniel as Matthew walked around the truck to meet them.

"What do I owe this surprise visit to?" he said as he reached out to shake Daniel's hand.

"I have some business to take care of in Sugarcreek and was hoping I could use one of the stable rooms in the top of the barn while I'm here. This is my friend, Matthew Byler. He has family in Sugarcreek and is going to visit with them while we're here."

"You're always welcome, and maybe I can get you to give me a hand while you're here. I'm short two hands and could use a couple of strong backs for a couple days." He slapped Daniel on the back. "Let's go sit a spell, and you can tell me all about life in Willow Springs."

As the three men crossed the yard heading to the porch, Matthew noticed the woman and *kinner* were no longer in the garden. The *kinner* were playing on the porch, but the woman was no longer outside that he could see.

Nathan was the first to reach the steps and asked the older woman if she would bring out something cold to drink.

She quickly rose out of her chair and set the bucket of beans she was snapping at her feet. Once Daniel got close enough to her, she smiled and said, "Daniel Miller, you're a sight for these old eyes. I never dreamed I'd see you again. It hasn't been the same since you've been gone. You always had a way of making this old woman laugh. I hope you'll stick around for a few days."

Daniel smiled and reached out to open the screen door for her as she walked by him to go get drinks. "I can't stay long, but I hope I get to at least enjoy a slice of your Dutch apple pie while I'm here."

Nathan pulled a couple of the rockers closer to the chair the woman had been sitting in and instructed the boys to sit down.

Daniel was the first to speak.

"Your mother looks good. Does she still cook every meal for the stable boys, and does she still make them take their boots off before they go in her kitchen?"

"This year's been hard on her. Ever since my *fraa* died, her health has gone downhill. She doesn't have as much energy as she used to, and it's hard for her to stand in the kitchen for very long. Sarah, my sister-in-law, helps with the cooking and cleaning as well as taking care of the *kinner*."

At the sound of him mentioning his sister-in-law's name, Matthew froze. He turned to Daniel and saw that he was looking back at him. Daniel started to say something, and Matthew quickly shook his head no. Daniel understood that Matthew didn't want him to say anything and let Nathan continue to talk about his mother's health.

"My *mamm* lives here in the main house with me, and my sister-in-law lives in the *doddi haus*. *Mamm* couldn't handle the *kinner* by herself anymore, so I sent for my sister-in-law to come help."

He turned to Matthew and said, "You may know her. My *fraa*'s family is from Willow Springs. Eli Mast owns the lumber mill there."

Matthew could feel the blood drain from his face. He couldn't believe what he was hearing. *Could it be possible that I walked right into where Sarah lived? Was she the woman I saw working in the garden?* It was all too much for him to absorb.

Just then, Nathan's mother came back out on the porch with a tray of tea and cookies. She placed the tray on the small table beside the door and started pouring cold drinks for them all.

"Daniel, how is your mother? Is she enjoying her home in Willow Springs? How does your father like his job? Is your mom still quilting?" She hardly took a breath between the questions she was hurling at him.

"Give the boy a chance to answer one question before you ask him another," Nathan said.

Daniel could hardly speak. He could see that Matthew was shaken and didn't want to single him out, so he tried to keep Nathan and his mother's attention by answering the questions she asked.

Matthew looked toward the *doddi haus*, hoping to see Sarah. He needed to calm his nerves and take in all that he had just learned.

"Nathan, do you mind if I take a walk around the stables? I've heard all of Daniel's stories, and I'd like to take a look at your farm." Matthew stood as he waited for Nathan to give him permission.

"Certainly, go enjoy yourself. Elijah is training some of our newest arrivals in the back pasture, if you want to go watch him."

Nathan's mother added that supper would be at six, and she'd set a couple extra places at the table so they could join them.

Matthew walked down the steps and headed toward the stables. He still couldn't believe what he'd just learned. For the past year he'd been wondering where Sarah was, now he was less than two hundred feet from her, and she didn't even know it. Now that he was here, he wasn't sure what he'd say to her. He had to clear his head and figure out what he was going to do.

What if she won't be happy to see me? he thought. *What if she found someone else? What if she and Nathan started making plans to marry? Why didn't she let me know where I could find her?*

The what-ifs were killing him. He couldn't even think of talking to her until he calmed the nerves that were raging inside him.

Daniel watched as his friend walked down the steps and headed to the stables. He couldn't believe they had walked right into finding Sarah. He hoped finding his sister would be just as easy.

Chapter 13

Finding Sarah

Sarah had been in the garden for hours when she glanced over her shoulder and noticed a truck pull down the driveway and stop in front of Nathan's house. It wasn't unusual for people to stop and talk to Nathan about his horses, and she just figured it was someone wanting to buy a new horse. At a quick glance, she noticed the passenger was an Amish man by his straw hat.

The garden was close enough to Nathan's house she could see when someone came, but far enough away, she really couldn't see who they were. Just as she was about to start picking more beans, the *kinner* were thirsty, and she guided them to the porch to play while she got them a drink.

Ever since she came to help Nathan and his mother, she lived in the small cottage across the yard from the main house. The bishop would never approve of her living in the main house with Nathan, so she lived here and tended to the *kinner* during the day. She helped Rosie with meals and the cleaning, but her primary concern was to look after her *schwester*'s *kinner*. The *kinner* needed her, and she'd fallen in love with them quickly. Amos was three and Rachel was four, and they both needed a *mamm*. It had been a year since she left Willow Springs, and her heart ached to go home, but she knew this is where *Gott* intended her to be.

Her thoughts drifted to Matthew and hoped he had found someone to love. The hardest thing she ever did was to decide not to let him know where he could find her. She knew the *kinner* needed her, and she knew Nathan had no desire to look for a *fraa* to help care for them. He was still mourning Susan, and even though he was twenty years older than her when they married, he handled the *kinner* like he was in his twenties.

Just that morning, she overheard Rosie tell him that it had been a year, and it was time he started looking for a new *fraa*. Rosie didn't think it was fair that she be responsible for raising her *schwester*'s *kinner* when she should be raising a family of her own. He said he waited a good long time to find Susan, and he was in no hurry to find another *fraa*. No one could ever compare to his Suzy.

Nathan was a good *datt* and tried his best to spend quality time with his *kinner*. Every evening when she returned to her cottage after supper, Nathan took over and made sure both had baths and were in bed at a decent hour.

It was those evening hours that she had to herself that she missed Matthew the most. She missed his letters, their buggy rides, the dimple in his chin, and, most of all, the plans they were making for their own life. They took lots of walks down by the creek behind the Byler Farm looking for the perfect place to build their new home. Matthew had the house all laid out with everything on her wish list checked off. It had a big wraparound porch just like his parents had, plenty of bedrooms to fill with *kinner*, and a huge room in the basement where she could open a dry goods store.

They had started to plan a life together, and she still couldn't believe she may never see him again. She had no way of knowing how long she would need to stay in Sugarcreek. Nathan and the *kinner* needed her more than she needed to return to Willow Springs. Or so she thought.

As she poured two glasses of milk and put a few cookies on a plate, she closed her eyes and tried to remember what Matthew looked like. She could still see his blue eyes and how they danced when he smiled, and she'd never forget the dimple in his chin. She prayed he was happy and moving on with his life. She needed to release him from the promises he'd made to her, but the thought of writing that letter was almost more than she could stand. She had to do it, but what was holding her back? Could it be she really didn't want to give up hope that he might be willing to wait for her?

She set the milk and cookies on the table and went to the door to call the *kinner* in for their snack. As she stood at the screen door, she could see the two men still on Nathan's porch. The visitors had their backs to her, so she couldn't tell if she recognized them. She loved to watch Nathan run his business; he took so much pride in making sure his customers had all their questions answered and matched them with the perfect horse.

"Aunt Sarah, after our snack can we go say hello to *Datt*?" Rachel asked as she took a bite of her cookie.

"It looks like he's talking business, so we best not bother him right now. If he's still on the porch after those men leave, we'll walk over to say hello. How does that sound?" she asked as she wiped milk from Amos's face.

Rosie had not been feeling well the last few months, so she tried to keep them out of her way. Most of their days were spent in the *doddi haus* or outside tending to the garden. She reached down and patted Amos on the top of the head and wiped off Rachel's milk mustache. She loved them as if they were her own. She knew at some point, Nathan would marry again, and she'd have to give up her role as their temporary mother; but for now, she loved them every bit as much as her *schwester* did.

"May we go back outside and play?" Rachel asked as she hopped down out of her chair.

"You may, but I want you to stay on the porch and don't wander off and go bother your *datt*," Sarah said as she wiped cookie crumbs from the table.

"I'll be back outside in a minute, and then we can finish picking that row of beans before I go help with supper."

She rinsed her hands in the sink and looked out the window to where Nathan and one of the men were still sitting on the porch. She wondered who he was and why they hadn't walked to the stables to look at the horses. One of the men was no longer sitting with them, and she assumed he'd already headed to the stables.

She grabbed the bucket beside the door and asked the *kinner* if they wanted to help her pick beans or stay on the porch playing with their wooden horses. She knew what the answer would be and was sure she'd be able to pick faster without them underfoot.

Matthew turned away from the *doddi haus* and headed straight to the stables. He had to find a spot where he could think and get his emotions under control. He walked through the double doors of the stable and right out the back door.

He stopped at the enclosed paddock and leaned on the fence attached to the back of the barn. From where he was standing, he could see all the pastures that surrounded the stables. To his left, he could barely see the back of the *doddi haus*, which was hidden by a large maple tree. The garden that ran alongside the smaller house was in full view. He noticed again how the sunflowers were in a neat row on the far side of the garden and how they all had their heads turned to the sun as they started to bloom.

He knew Sarah loved flowers and bet she was the one responsible for making sure the garden was filled with bright and colorful blooms. He leaned his head down on his arms that were crossed and leaning on the fence rail. He closed his eyes and instantly remembered a conversation he and Sarah had about sunflowers.

It was late one evening after he'd brought her home from a *singeon*. He pulled his buggy alongside the barn of her *datt's* sawmill. He positioned the buggy so they could look out into the meadow beside the creek that ran right through their property. Her *mamm's* garden was planted with row after row of sunflowers.

"Sunflowers amaze me. I just love how they follow the warmth of the sun, and they always look like they are smiling at me. They were my *mamm's* favorite flower. We plant them every year just like she would have done, if she were still living. Once in a while, I see my *datt* standing in the garden all by himself. He says they had some of their best conversations in the garden, and that's where he can feel her the most."

"Matthew, when we have a garden of our own, can we make sure there is always room for sunflowers?"

"We can plant the whole garden with sunflowers, if that would make you happy."

That memory seemed so long ago. He should have known it was her garden the minute he pulled into the driveway and saw it lined with sunflowers. He lifted his head just in time to see her walk through the gate and sit down at the end of a row, bucket in hand. He stayed there looking at her for what seemed like hours. He couldn't believe he was that close to her and so lost for words. He never had any trouble talking to her before, why was he having so much trouble going to her now?

As Sarah started to pick beans, she had the strange feeling of being watched. She looked over to the porch where Nathan and his visitor were sitting, and they looked like they were still deep in conversation. She turned to look at the *kinner*, and they were playing with their toys on the porch. There was no one else around, but she couldn't shake the feeling of someone watching her.

Turning her attention back to picking beans, her thoughts went back to Matthew.

Why is he so fresh on my mind today? she thought. *Is* Gott *trying to tell me I need to write to him? Why is it so difficult to write that letter?*

She was still in love with him, and down deep, she didn't want to let him go. Just the thought of him finding someone else brought fresh tears to her eyes. She ached to see his blue eyes looking back at her. All her dreams were shattered the day her *schwester* died in that buggy accident.

She felt it was time she asked Nathan if she could go home for a few days. She hadn't received a letter from her *datt* in weeks, and it was time she went and faced Matthew. Questions were spinning in her head.

Is there a way we could make this work? Would Matthew ever consider moving to Sugarcreek so I could take care of the kinner? Any thought of that quickly got pushed away with remembering how much Matthew loved to farm. They had talked about building a house down near the creek, and he told her more than once he never wanted to leave Willow Springs. *How am I ever going to live without him?*

Her eyes were clouded with tears, and she was having trouble seeing the beans she was picking. She quickly pulled herself together before the *kinner* noticed she was crying and started asking questions. Just as she began to stand up to walk to the other side of the row, she heard footsteps behind her. She turned to see who was coming, but the afternoon sun was blinding her as she turned toward the sound.

All she could see was a tall, dark man dressed in Amish clothing. She lifted her hand to shade the glare of the sun when the blue eyes she'd been daydreaming of were looking back at her. Her heart skipped a beat as he said her name.

"Sarah."

"Matthew, is that really you?"

The weight of the world came crashing down, and she stumbled as she tried to move toward him. He reached out to catch her as she collapsed into his arms. She couldn't believe he was standing in front of her.

Is he the man I saw getting out of the truck a little bit ago, and why is he here? she thought. She wanted to ask him a hundred questions, but all she could do was bury her head in his chest.

If he'd ever suspected she'd found someone else, his questions were quickly answered as she wrapped her arms around him. He looked over the top of her head toward the porch, not wanting anyone to see them embrace. He guided her to the corner of the house so they could have some privacy. Once he had her shielded from view, he took his hands and placed them on each side of her face. He leaned his forehead in to meet hers and stood bonded like that for a few seconds.

"What are you doing here? How did you find me?"

"I came here with Daniel Miller, and while we were talking to Nathan, I realized he was your brother-in-law and his *fraa* was Susan."

"Did you tell Nathan you knew me?"

"No, he thinks I'm off looking at the horses. I had to walk away and get my thoughts together before I found you. I have so many questions, but right now, I just want to look at you. I've missed you, and life hasn't been the same since you left.

"I checked the mail every day, hoping for a letter. You promised you'd write. I don't understand why I haven't heard from you."

"When I first got here, Amos had stopped talking and all Rachel did was cry. They missed their *mamm* so much, it took me months to get them back to normal. Nathan walked around in shock and spent most of his days with the horses. His mother missed Susan as well, and her health has been getting worse each day.

"I was so busy, and everyone needed me so much, I just couldn't give you an answer to when I might be able to come home. Nathan has no desire to marry again, and I didn't think I'd be able to leave the *kinner. Gott* sent me here to take care of them, and my life had to take second to their needs. I didn't feel it was fair holding you to the promises and plans we had started to make. I'd meant to write to you and release you from those promises but just couldn't find the words."

"So, you haven't found anyone else?"

"Oh, Matthew, of course not."

He pulled her close and whispered in her ear, "Then could it be you couldn't write that letter because you really didn't want to let me go?" He wrapped his arms around her tighter as she laid her head on his shoulder.

She knew right then that he was the man *Gott* intended her to share her life with; and somehow, someway, they would make it work.

"Aunt Sarah, where are you?" Rachel hollered from the porch.

She pushed herself away and said, "The *kinner* need me."

Before he could say another word, she turned and walked away before they came looking for her. Just as she got to the corner of the house, she turned around and said, "Please don't say anything to Nathan yet."

He just stood there looking at her. *What am I going to do now?*

He needed her, the *kinner* needed her, Nathan's mother needed her, and by the sounds of it, Nathan needed her. He sat down on the ground and leaned up against the side of the house. With his head in his hands, he prayed to *Gott*, something he hadn't done too much of lately.

"*Gott*, you know my heart. Sarah is the girl for me, and I've missed her. If it's in your will, please help me find a way to make a life with her."

Nathan stood up and looked out over the farm and toward the horse stables. "I wonder where Matthew is?"

"I'm sure he's enjoying his walk. It's been a while since we ate dinner, and I'm sure once he knows it's getting close to suppertime, he'll find his way back." Daniel said as he kicked his feet out straight to make himself more comfortable.

Just then, he saw Nathan's children running across the driveway and hollering as they came up the steps.

"*Datt*, look what we found in the garden today," Rachel said as she pushed a coffee can up under his nose.

In the can were two caterpillars clinging for their life on a small tree branch that had been propped up with clumps of grass.

"Well I'll be, it looks like you made a nice home for your friends," Nathan said.

Coming up the steps behind them was Sarah carrying a basket of freshly picked green beans. Daniel noticed that she looked upset and wondered if she and Matthew had spoken. Nathan didn't seem to notice her flushed face, but Daniel noticed right away.

"Do you mind if the *kinner* sit on the porch with you for a few minutes while I go help your *mamm* with supper?" she asked. He picked up Amos and tossed him in the air like a rag doll.

"Do I mind? I'd like nothing more than to spend some time with my favorite *kinner*."

It had taken Amos months to start talking again after Susan died, and when he did, he began to call her *mamm*. She didn't have the heart to correct him, and Nathan agreed that he didn't find any harm in letting him continue. Rachel called her Aunt Sarah from the very beginning and never once called her anything else.

She opened the screen door and turned to look over at the *kinner* crawling on their *datt*'s lap. *How am I ever going to tell Matthew I can't leave them?*

Chapter 14

Crayfish

Winded and needing to sit, Rosie pulled out a chair behind Sarah and started to slice a loaf of bread for supper.

Peering at Sarah over the wire-rimmed glasses she wore low on her nose she said, "Daniel brought a boy with him from Willow Springs. I think he said his name was Matthew Byler. Do you know him? Seems like a nice enough fellow, didn't talk much, and he took off somewhere shortly after they got here, and we haven't seen hide nor hair of him since."

"Sarah, are you listening to me? You're looking out the window like you've lost your best friend. What's got you so quiet this afternoon?"

"I guess I'm missing home today," she said as she busied herself getting the ham ready to slice for sandwiches.

When she glanced out the window and saw Matthew come from around the stable and head for the porch, shivers ran up her arms as she watched him walk across the yard. He always walked with so much confidence, but today, his shoulders were sagging. She figured she was the cause of his posture and wished she could've spent more time with him before the *kinner* called her away. She had to find a way to be alone with him again.

Her mind was racing, and she didn't want Nathan to know about them yet. If he knew, he'd send her home, and she didn't want to leave the *kinner*. She couldn't imagine he'd ever stand in her way of having a family of her own if he knew she was in love with Matthew. She felt an obligation to care for her *schwester*'s *kinner*. Why did everything have to be so hard to figure out? She couldn't take care of the *kinner* in Willow Springs, and she couldn't be Matthew's *fraa* in Sugarcreek.

Matthew walked up on the porch and sat in the chair next to Nathan. Daniel wanted to ask him if he'd spoken to Sarah, but by the look on his face, he was sure he had.

"So, what do you think of the place?" Nathan asked.

"I've never seen a spread quite like this before. You have so many horses and all at different levels of training. The farmhands look like they keep the place in tip-top shape, and they all look like they know exactly what they're doing."

Nathan stood up and put Amos on the floor next to Rachel and said, "It takes a lot of hands to run this place, and right now I could use a few more. How do you both feel about earning your room and board by giving me a hand after supper? I have a fence that needs mending in the north pasture that I've been trying to get to all day."

Daniel was the first to speak up.

"I think I can wait until tomorrow to start looking for my sister if Matthew can wait until then to visit his aunt."

Matthew just nodded. He hadn't even given his aunt another thought since his mind was full of Sarah.

Daniel had filled Nathan in that afternoon on his plans to find his sister.

"I think that would be a great idea. I could use some hard work to clear my head," Matthew said as he reached for a cookie on the stand beside his chair.

"Now don't go filling up on cookies, Sarah and Rosie will be calling us for supper soon, and Rosie's a great cook. It's the one thing I miss the most around here," Daniel mentioned.

Matthew's heart skipped a beat with just the thought of going inside where Sarah was. *How am I ever going to sit down to a meal and not talk openly to her?* he thought.

He didn't understand why she was so adamant about Nathan not knowing about them. He seemed like an understanding man and was sure if he knew the plans they had, he'd let her return home. He was just going to have to find a way to talk to her again and try to get her to tell Nathan.

Turning toward Matthew, Nathan asked, "So, tell me about yourself. You seem pretty interested in farming. What do you do in Willow Springs?"

"My *datt* runs a furniture shop, and I work the farm. I grow corn and soybeans that I sell to the Feed & Seed every fall. I just finished with all my spring planting and I'm just watching the fields grow now.

"In between planting and harvesting, I've been raising bottle calves to sell to farmers who want to raise them for beef. I've had some trouble the last six months with dying calves. My *datt* and I finally figured out I was poisoning them with water from old lead pipes. It's really Daniel's fault."

"My fault? How is dying livestock my fault?"

"I guess I forgot to tell you that we figured it out. Remember last winter when you got the feed truck stuck beside the barn? The weight of the truck busted the new water line, and the ground had been too frozen for me to fix it. I wasn't too worried since I knew I could draw water from the old well into the barn.

"My *datt* forgot to tell me that those old pipes were lead and that is why they laid new lines years ago. The lines that ran to the house and alpaca barn were separate, and I only had to shut off the lines to the barn when you got the truck stuck. I'd meant to fix them once spring came, but I got busy planting, and I didn't give it another thought."

"Well, I guess it was my fault then." Daniel said.

"I got all the pipes replaced, and the water turned back on in the barn when Daniel asked me to come to Sugarcreek. I decided I needed a break before I figure out what I want to do next. I'm not too sure I want to take on more calves. I'm interested in what you're doing here with these horses and would like to learn more about your operation."

"There's no better way to learn than to dig right in. I could always use a good farmhand if you're interested in sticking around until your crops need to be harvested. If you catch on quick, I'm looking for a farm in Willow Springs where I can winter horses at. I have a lot of business up your way and could use a holding farm in your area.

"We would do the initial training here, and then once they're ready to be sold, we'd truck them to your farm. It would help my buyers in the north if they had a local farm they could travel to instead of hiring drivers to bring them here." Nathan was hopeful Matthew was interested in his proposal.

"That's an interesting thought. I'd need to talk it over with my *datt* and see what he thinks, but we may be able to work something out. I hadn't planned on staying in Sugarcreek for more than a week, but this might be a good idea. My Aunt Anna Mae lives nearby, and my *datt* wanted me to check in on her."

"Anna Mae Troyer?" Nathan asked.

"Yes, why, do you know her?"

"Know her? She lives down the road from here and is in my church district. Why don't you both plan on going to church with us in the morning and you can see her then?"

"Well, this trip is getting easier and easier. I think that's a great idea. What do you think, Daniel? Are you up for an Amish church service tomorrow?" Matthew asked.

"I am always up for church, and it's been a long time since I've gone. I used to go with Nathan when I worked here, and it would be good to see some of my old friends." Daniel smiled as he reminisced about his time he spent working with Nathan.

"It's a plan. We'll leave about eight o'clock. Service is not too far from here this week," Nathan said.

Just as they finished up talking, Rosie came to the screen door and mentioned supper was on the table. She instructed the *kinner* to go get washed up and asked Nathan if he could bring in the tray when he came in.

"It doesn't matter how old I get, I swear that woman will always boss me around like I'm twelve," Nathan said with a big smile on his face. And he did what she asked and gathered up the glasses, pitcher, and plate of cookies before he headed inside.

Three of the farmhands had come in the side door promptly at six o'clock and took their seats at the table. By the way they took their seats, they had regular places at the table. Nathan took a few minutes to introduce Matthew and Daniel and then went on asking them about some of the jobs he had them working on that day.

Matthew was nervous about being so close to Sarah and lingered, so he was the last one to come to the table. Once everyone had sat down, there was only one chair that was available, and it was right next to Sarah.

The commotion around the table was like any other typical family setting. The *kinner* were anxious to start eating, and Sarah had to instruct them to sit still and behave. It only took one stern look from Nathan for them both to settle down and use their manners. Nathan bowed his head for a silent prayer, and all those around the table did the same.

Sarah could hardly breathe. She couldn't believe Matthew was sitting so close, and she had to act like she barely knew him. He was so close but still so far away. She wasn't sure how the whole room couldn't feel the tension between them.

Nathan cleared his throat to indicate the prayer was over, and they could start eating.

"After supper, I am putting these two to work in the north pasture fixing fence with me. We had a good visit this afternoon, but it's time to get some work done before the sun sets," Nathan stated as he reached for the platter of ham sandwiches.

After Nathan took a sandwich, he put one on his *kinner's* plates and then handed it to Sarah. Her hands were shaking, and it was the first time Nathan had looked her in the eye all afternoon.

"Sarah, you're shaking. Are you feeling ill? You don't look yourself today," Nathan said.

"She's been awful quiet all afternoon. She told me she was missing Willow Springs, but I think it's more than that," Rosie commented.

"I think it's because Daniel and Matthew are here and are reminding me of home. I haven't heard from my *datt* in a couple weeks, and that worries me."

"Do you boys know Eli Mast?" Nathan asked. He owns the lumber mill in Willow Springs."

Matthew lifted his head and looked right at Daniel, not sure what to say. He knew Sarah didn't want Nathan knowing just how well they knew each other, and he didn't want Daniel to say anything that might give it away.

Daniel didn't say a word as he waited for Matthew to answer. He could see the panicked look in his eyes and needed to question him about it later.

"I know Eli. I saw him last Sunday, and he looked well. He never stays for the meal after church, so I don't get a chance to speak to him much," Matthew stated.

"So, you and Sarah were in the same church district? Did you go to school together? Did you know my Susan?" Nathan was anxious to hear all about his late *fraa*'s family in Willow Springs.

"Yes, to all of your questions. I was surprised to see Sarah today. I knew she moved to Sugarcreek."

Matthew was pleased he was able to answer all of Nathan's questions without stretching the truth or letting on how close he and Sarah really were.

"Well, I bet the two of you have a lot of catching up to do. It'd be good for Sarah to hear all about her family and friends in Willow Springs. Since she's so homesick today, maybe the two of you can spend some time catching up later. How about I take one of the other farmhands with Daniel and me to fix the fence and you can let Sarah know what's going on at home?"

Nathan was pleased that he might be able to ease her homesickness by suggesting she spend time with Matthew. He knew Sarah had left all of her family to come help him with the *kinner*. He hated to admit it, but he had to agree with his mother that it wasn't fair that she be tied down when she needed to be starting a family of her own.

Sarah didn't know what to say, so she busied herself with filling the *kinner*'s plates with green beans and potato salad. She wanted to talk to Matthew but didn't want Rosie around when she did. She knew if they spent time out on the porch, Rosie and the *kinner* would be right there with them.

She passed the bowl of potatoes to Matthew as she asked, "I promised to take the *kinner* for a walk after supper. Would you like to come with us?"

"I think that's a great idea as long as Nathan is sure he doesn't need my help with the fence," Matthew stated as he turned to Nathan for his answer.

"Like I said, I can get one of the other hands to help, right, boys?" Nathan said as he turned his attention to the three farmhands at the other end of the table.

Rachel waited her turn to talk and then asked, "Can we walk to the creek and go wading?"

Matthew couldn't help but smile at the girl's excitement about the creek.

"I think that sounds like fun. I haven't been wading in years. What do you say, Sarah, are you up for crayfish to tickle your toes?" Matthew said.

At that, Amos started to laugh.

"Can we take my bucket and catch crayfish?" Amos asked.

"Now, wait a minute. This is starting to sound like too much fun. Maybe I had better rethink this. How about Matthew goes and fix the fence and I go wading in the creek?" Nathan said with a big smile on his face.

Sarah felt the blood rush from her face. She wanted to talk to Matthew alone, and going for a walk was the perfect solution.

Nathan immediately saw the disappointed look in Sarah's eyes and said, "Don't worry, I was just joking. I think it would be good for you to talk to Matthew about home. You and the *kinner* go for your walk and catch some crayfish."

As Rosie turned her attention to Sarah, she said, "Then it's settled. After supper, you take the *kinner* for a walk, and I'll clean up the kitchen."

"Don't be silly. I can help you do that first. I'd hate to leave this all to you," Sarah said.

"Child, I've cleaned up more dishes than I care to count, and it won't hurt me to do it myself just this once. We need to get that forlorn look off your face, and if hearing about home will help, then that's just what the doctor ordered."

Rosie's tone was one Sarah knew not to argue with, so she just nodded and went back to eating her supper.

Nathan kept the conversation going as he went back to asking the farmhands about the jobs they were working on. Daniel was so confused by the casual way Matthew and Sarah were acting. He knew Matthew loved her just by the way he talked about her on their ride to Sugarcreek. Why were they keeping it a big secret? He shook his head and figured Matthew would tell him what he wanted to know later.

It wasn't long before Nathan pushed his chair back, stood up, and stated that it was time to get back to work. Daniel followed suit, as did the farmhands at the end of the table. The *kinner* eagerly asked if they could go for their walk now, and Sarah stood to start cleaning off the table.

"Let me help clear off the table and get the dishes started, and I'll be ready to go. Why don't you both take Matthew outside and show him the new kittens under the porch? I'll be out in a few minutes," she said as she carried a stack of dishes to the sink.

Rachel jumped out of her chair and went around to where Matthew was sitting and grabbed his hand and said, "Come on. I'll show you where the kittens are. There are five of them and we have them named already."

"Wait for me," Amos hollered.

Nathan wiped his face and picked him up out of his chair and put him on the floor so he could run after his *schwester*.

Rosie cleared her throat and said, "I'm plenty capable of cleaning up the kitchen by myself. You do your fair share around here, and it's fine time you take an evening off. Nathan works you too hard anyways. Go enjoy yourself."

She reached to pour herself a cup of coffee and said, "I'm going to sit right here for a few more minutes, and then I'll take care of this kitchen."

Sarah knew not to argue with her, but she finished clearing the table anyways.

It wasn't long, and she was grabbing her shoes from the back porch and heading around front to meet up with Matthew and the *kinner*. When she rounded the house, she saw three bodies lying on the ground, all propped up on their elbows, peering under the porch.

"Aunt Sarah, they have their eyes open now," Rachel squealed.

"They do? It won't be long now, and they'll start to venture out from underneath the porch, and then you'll get to hold them," Sarah said as she lay down on the grass to look as well.

"That's if momma cat lets you. They get pretty protective. She may not let them out of her sight for a while," Matthew said.

Sarah lay right next to Matthew on the ground and looked under the porch to get a closer look.

Matthew turned his head to look at her and found she was close enough he could smell the faint scent of lilacs. He knew that smell, her smell—the smell of flowers and sunshine. He continued to look at her, but she had her full attention on the mother and her kittens.

The *kinner* were busy counting the kittens, and he was enjoying lying right in the middle of them all. It felt so natural being here with her. It was the same peace he felt whenever he was around her in Willow Springs. But he wasn't in Willow Springs, and he wasn't free to court Sarah in Sugarcreek. How was he ever going to let her out of his sight again? He knew one thing for sure—they had to figure out a solution to this problem.

Maybe he'd take Nathan up on his offer to stick around for a couple months and learn about the horse business. He hoped Sarah would be receptive to the idea, and better yet, he hoped his *datt* would agree to use the farm as a holding stable for Nathan's horses.

"Well, *kinner*, if we want to go wading in the creek before it gets dark, we'd better get going," Sarah said as she stood up and brushed the grass off her dress.

"If we're going wading, why did you bring your shoes?" Rachel asked.

"You're right. No need for shoes today. It's warm enough, and I think a walk to the creek is just what we all need," Sarah said.

"In that case, I guess I'd better get these work boots off myself," Matthew said as he pushed himself up to a sitting position and started to take off his boots.

As they began to walk down the lane toward the creek, the *kinner* ran off in front of them, chasing butterflies. Once they got to the end of the path, they turned into the meadow and walked along the side of the fence that surrounded the pasture. In the field, a dozen horses were grazing on the fresh green grass.

"It's beautiful here," Matthew said.

"I've fallen in love with it here, but more importantly, I've fallen in love with the *kinner*. I miss Susan so much and taking care of her *kinner* has helped me deal with losing her. My *mamm* was sick for so long and died when I was little, so I know what it's like to not have a *mamm*. I just can't let Rachel and Amos face that alone.

"My *datt* never remarried, and we needed a *mamm*. I just don't have it in me to leave them. I know it was wrong of me not to write to you, but please understand I couldn't leave them. I couldn't figure out how to have a life with you and still take care of them," Sarah's voice was cracking as she explained it to him.

"If only you would've told me and not left me to wonder what had happened to you, we could've come up with a solution together. I thought you knew I wanted to make a life with you, and that means facing challenges together. You left me out to face them by yourself. I thought you wanted a life with me as well?" he asked.

"I do, and there were days I couldn't think of anything else, but I just couldn't figure out how to make it work. I knew you'd never leave your farm, and again, I couldn't leave the *kinner*."

He reached for her hand to help her over a tree that had fallen across the path and said, "You underestimate me. If there's a will, there's always a way."

She missed the feel of his hand in hers, and the electric charge that happened between them when they touched made her instantly feel he would make it work. The *kinner* had run on ahead, already knowing the way to the creek. They were all alone on the path for a few minutes.

As she stepped over the log, he grabbed her other hand and was standing directly in front of her and said, "You have to trust me. I'll find a way we can be together. I've not dreamed and worried about you for the past year to let you out of my sight again. I'm not sure how at this exact moment, but you need to trust me enough that I'll figure it out. I have some things to work through, but my plans are for you to be my *fraa*, if you'll still have me."

"Have you? It's all I have ever wanted…that was until Rachel and Amos came into the picture. I've prayed every day that *Gott* would show me what to do. I know it's His will that I'm here, and He has a reason for everything and that I don't question."

He lifted her chin so she could look into his eyes.

"Listen to me. We have a lot to discuss, and I have a lot to sort out, but I'm here, and I'm not leaving Sugarcreek until we find a way to make this work."

"I don't want Nathan to know about us. I don't want to put pressure on him to marry or to send me back to Willow Springs. I couldn't bear leaving the *kinner*."

"For now, I'll agree to keep Nathan from knowing about our plans, but I'm not promising that we won't tell him at some point. Do you understand that?" he asked.

"I do," she said.

At that, they heard the *kinner* calling their names, and he quickly dropped her hands and started walking down the path toward them. Once they got to the clearing, the creek was in plain sight, and the kids took off running toward the water.

"Should we stop them?" he asked.

"No, the creek is only a foot deep right here, and the only concern we have is how many crayfish are going to pinch their toes." She started to run, challenging him to race her to the creek.

He let her take off first and watched her run toward the water. He could see the love she had for them and knew she'd be a wonderful *mamm* to their own *kinner* someday. He had much to think about, but right now, he was going to enjoy just being near her again.

Chapter 15

Church in Sugarcreek

It was early Sunday morning, and Matthew woke from a sound sleep. He couldn't remember the last time he'd slept so well. Even the lumpy cot couldn't damper his spirits. He lay quiet for a few minutes, remembering how beautiful Sarah looked in the garden yesterday. He couldn't believe he'd found her. Knowing she was safe helped him sleep well. He swung his feet over the end of the bed, grabbed his boots, and tiptoed to the door trying not to wake Daniel. It was dark, and he tripped on Daniel's boots and fell face first on the floor with a big thud.

"So much for being quiet," he mumbled under his breath.

Daniel sat straight up in bed and hollered, "What was that?"

Matthew picked himself up off the floor and stumbled back to the cot.

"That was me trying to be quiet so I didn't wake you. How'd I do?"

"I thought it was the horses in the barn. I'm glad it was just you. Where are you going so early?"

"I thought I'd go down and help get an early start with the chores before we go to church."

"You sneaking downstairs so early doesn't have anything to do with you hoping to see Sarah, does it?"

Matthew didn't answer him right away and tried to change the subject by asking him what time they needed to leave for church.

"Nathan said last night that service is at the neighbors', so we don't need to leave until eight. We have plenty of time to get breakfast and help with chores."

Matthew reached for his boots and busied himself with putting them on, while Daniel stood up and stretched the sleep away.

"What are your plans for the day?" Matthew asked.

"I figured I'd dig out the address after church, and we could try to find it. I'm sure if it's an Amish family, they'll talk to me easier if I have you with me."

"Of course. I hope we find something you can use today. I hate to think we drove all this way for nothing," Matthew said.

"Even if I don't find Elizabeth, the trip will be worth it, just because you found Sarah. I've never seen you smile so much. It looked like you had a great time last night playing with the children and catching up with Sarah. So, what are you going to do now that you've found her? I'm surprised you didn't say anything to Nathan. Why are you acting like you barely know one another when I know that's not true?"

"I'm not sure what we're going to do yet, but I did promise her I wouldn't say anything to Nathan just yet. She's afraid he'll send her back to Willow Springs, if he knows we had plans to marry. She feels responsible for taking care of them, and she can't bear the thought of leaving them. I can see she loves them. I'm not sure what to do. Right now, I am going to give it some thought, take it to the Lord, and pray He'll show me the answer."

He finished tying his boots and stood up and walked toward the door.

"After we go find your address, can we stop and check on my aunt? Nathan said she doesn't live too far from here, and we might see her at church if she's feeling well. He told me last night she's been under the weather and hasn't been attending church regularly."

"You bet," Daniel said as he followed Matthew out the door.

They walked side by side as they went down the steps from the loft and into the stables. The sun was just starting to peek up over the horizon, and the light was coming in the double doors at the far end of the stable. They both stood there, taking in the beautiful sight. You could hear the horses starting to stir as they stood there.

"This is my favorite time of the day in the barn. During the summer, they leave the doors open, and if you come downstairs at the right moment, it will look like the sun is coming through the doors and landing in the middle of the barn."

"I remember once a farmhand walked in from the back of the stables through those doors. With the sun shining in, it looked like he was walking out of the sun. Pretty amazing, isn't it?"

Daniel slapped Matthew on the back, grabbed the wheelbarrow and shovel, and said, "This is a good place to start while we wait for the others to get up."

Matthew walked up behind him, and grabbed another wheelbarrow and shovel, and went to the opposite side of the barn. As he walked to the first stall, he looked at the name written in chalk on the board outside the stall door.

NAME: Sir Philip

TEMPERAMENT: Nervous

Sir Philip had pinned his ears back close to his neck and looked Matthew's way as he unlatched the door and reached for the lead. He stood still as he quietly talked to him.

"I'm just going to stand here until you get used to me. I bet you'd like to go outside for some fresh air?"

The horse started to snort and backed into the corner of the stall, stomping his front hoof on the ground.

From across the barn, one of the farm hands hollered, "Be careful with that one! His last handler had a mean streak, and he doesn't like men. The only person that can calm him down is Sarah."

Matthew kept his eyes on the horse as he continued to talk. In a whisper he said, "While isn't that something? Sarah's the only one that can calm me down as well. We should get along just fine then, don't ya think?"

From behind him, he heard the gate open but didn't dare take his eyes off the horse while the person relatched the gate and stood behind him.

He stood there for a few minutes, looking the horse straight in the eye and not moving a muscle. In an instant, the horse relaxed his ears and started to move in his direction. Only then did he turn his head to see who had come into the stall.

Sarah moved closer, with her hand extended, to offer the horse a sugar cube.

"He's got a sweet tooth and is adamant about not leaving his stall until he gets his morning treat."

She grabbed the lead from Matthew's hand, clipped it to Sir Philip's halter, and led him out of the stall.

Matthew stood in awe of the instant transformation the horse showed when it saw Sarah.

It wasn't long before he heard a bell ring in the distance, signaling it was time for breakfast. Matthew had just finished emptying his wheelbarrow and was lining it up with the others when Daniel shouted.

"My second favorite part of the day is Rosie's breakfast."

They walked alongside the other farmhands headed to the house. Each of them stopped at the back door to remove their boots before they walked inside.

"Rosie is a stickler about dirty boots in her kitchen. She's trained us well." Daniel laughed as he waited his turn.

Matthew was the last in line as he walked into the kitchen. All the chairs had been filled, except the one right next to Sarah again. He pulled the chair out and sat down, and she turned to him and gave him a warm hello. He smiled, nodded his head, and scooted his chair closer to the table.

Nathan had his hands full getting Amos situated in his chair, and Rosie was helping Rachel tie a towel around her neck so she didn't get her church dress sticky from breakfast.

Sarah quietly asked Matthew if he wanted a cup of coffee, and before he could answer, she was filling his cup. Nathan finally sat down and said good morning to everyone. He quickly bowed his head for the silent prayer, and everyone followed suit.

Sarah closed her eyes and placed her hands in her lap to thank *Gott* for bringing Matthew to her. Her heart was overjoyed with him being so near. She instantly felt at peace, something she hadn't felt in a long time.

As soon as she closed her eyes, she felt Matthew lay his hand over hers. He only left it there for a split second but long enough that she felt the warmth and his love through the gentle squeeze he gave her hand. Before she had time to respond, he removed it.

She felt the air leave her lungs, and she heard herself gasp at his bold show of affection. Before she could give it more thought, Nathan had cleared his throat, signaling prayer was over. She was the last to raise her head and open her eyes, and when she did, Rosie was looking her way.

"Are you okay, child? I thought I heard you sigh."

"I'm all right," she said as she took a pancake off the platter and passed it to Matthew.

As she turned in her chair, her thigh brushed up against his leg. She had yet to recover from the touch of his hand when she felt the warmth of his thigh touch hers. She quickly pulled her leg away, and when she did, he moved his so they were touching again.

Every time she moved to release the magnetic pull he had on her, he moved his leg closer so he could feel her even in the slightest way. Realizing she couldn't move anymore to the left or she'd fall out of her chair, she gave in to his touch. She had a hard time swallowing, so she put her fork down and concentrated on sipping her cup of coffee instead.

The friendly bantering the farmhands were making about her calming Sir Philip down made her smile. They teased Matthew about her having to come to his rescue and what would have happened if she didn't come along.

At that exact moment, Amos spilled his milk, and she jumped up to grab a towel. Nathan turned the cup over as she wiped up the spilled milk and carried it to the sink. She needed a few minutes to collect herself, so she busied herself rinsing the towel.

By the time she had returned to her chair, everyone else had just about cleaned their plates.

Nathan was the first to finish, and he pushed himself away from the table as he said, "I'm going to go change and get the buggies ready. We'll leave for church in twenty minutes. Daniel, you and Matthew can take the cart that's parked behind the stable. Hook Ester up to it. She's still in training and needs the practice. That is, if you think you can handle her?"

Daniel was excited; Nathan knew he loved that cart.

Matthew excused himself from the table and headed to the loft to change. Just as he finished, he could hear Daniel running up the stairs, taking them two at a time.

"You don't mind going to an Amish service?" Matthew asked as he watched Daniel come through the door.

"I went all the time when I worked here. That's one of Nathan's stipulations if you work and stay in the loft. Church service isn't an option—it's a requirement. I got to know a lot of his neighbors, and it was hard to leave everyone when my dad took the job in Pittsburgh. I went so much, I understood some of the sermons, or at least I learned some of the High German words."

Sarah didn't have time to think about Matthew; she had her hands full getting the pies in the buggy and keeping the *kinner* from getting too dirty before church. Rosie had already climbed up in the buggy and was waiting for Sarah to hand Amos up to her. Just as she turned around to pick Amos up, Matthew and Daniel walked out of the stable and headed around back to get the cart.

Just the sight of him in his black hat and church clothes made her heart skip a beat. She laughed at herself and shook her head, thinking that she was worse than a schoolgirl with a silly schoolgirl crush. Still smiling, she handed Amos up to Rosie and climbed up in the front scat next to Rachel.

"What are you smiling about Aunt Sarah? Did you see something funny?" Rachel asked as she looked up at her so innocently.

"Nothing important, sweetie, I just remembered something that's all."

"You sure have been acting mighty funny this morning," Rosie said as she shook her head side to side.

Just then, Nathan climbed up and asked if everyone was ready. He picked up the reins, slapped them on the back of his horse, and guided him to turn the buggy around so they could go down the long lane that led to the road.

Behind them followed the three carts with the farmhands in two and Matthew and Daniel in the other.

Matthew was amazed at how well Daniel could handle the horse and the cart.

"If I didn't know better, I'd think you drove carts, not cars," Matthew said with a smile on his face.

They rode in silence as Daniel hummed a tune and Matthew took in the sights of the country. As they drove down the road, Matthew noticed the road signs as they passed.

When they came to Troyer Lane, he said, "Hey, that's the road my aunt lives on. She doesn't live too far from Nathan at all."

"That's good. We can stop on our way home this afternoon, and then once we get back to the stable, we can trade this cart for my truck and go see what we can find out about Elizabeth."

"Sounds like a plan," Matthew said.

They only rode for about fifteen minutes before they saw Nathan turn into a farm on the right-hand side of the road. There were already over twenty buggies lined up against the fence, and you could see young boys unhitching the horses and leading them to the corral out back.

Women were carrying dishes into the house, and the men were gathering outside by the barn. By the looks of it, service was going to be held inside the barn. Both double doors were wide open. Benches had been added and lined up in neat rows facing each other. As the members started to file inside, the women and girls sat on one side, and the men and boys sat on the other.

A hardcovered *Ausbund* hymnbook lay on the spot on the benches. Most of the church members never opened the book and knew the songs by memory. As the women started to take their places, the older women went in first, followed by the younger women and single girls. Sarah and Rachel sat in the second to the last row.

A few minutes before nine, the men started to file in. The men sat opposite the women, and Sarah watched as each of them took their seats. She patiently waited, trying not to look obvious, as she looked and watched for Matthew to take his place. Since he was not a member of this district, he came in last, and by then, the benches were filled. He stood at the back of the barn next to Daniel and leaned up against the wall. Once he got settled, he lifted his head and looked around the room to see where Sarah had sat. When he saw her, he smiled and removed his hat from his head and turned his attention to the song leader.

The service started when the vorsinger sang the first few notes of the first song. As they began to sing, the ministers stood from their seats in the front row and walked out the open doors at the front of the barn. There they would decide who was going to preach and wouldn't return to the service until near the end of the singing.

Daniel missed this part of an Amish service the most. He loved hearing how each note was sung slow and with meaning. He attended the Amish service so many times that he knew the second song was always number 770 in the *Ausbund*, "Lob Lied." He asked Nathan to translate the twenty-minute song for him and worked hard to memorize it. Nathan explained that in every service across the country, the song was sung second and was the most treasured song among the Amish. He quietly sang the song, which he translated into English to himself, as he looked around the room at the familiar faces.

Lob Lieb or "Praise Song"

O God, Father, we exalt you,
And praise your goodness,
Which you, Oh Lord, so graciously
Have demonstrated to us anew.
You, Lord, have brought us together
To exhort us by means of your Word.
Grant us grace to this end.
Open the mouth, Lord, of your servant,
And besides, grant him wisdom
That he may speak your Word aright,
Such as promotes a pious life
And is useful to your praise.

Give us a hunger for such nourishment;
This is our desire.
Give our hearts, also, understanding
And enlightment here on earth,
So that our Word may become familiar to us
That we might become pious,
And live in the righteousness,
Heeding your Word at all times.
Thus, one remains undeceived.
The kingdom, O Lord, is yours alone,
And the power likewise, the same.
We exalt you in the assembly,
And glorify thy name,
Entreating from our heart's depths
That you would be with us in this hour.
Through Jesus Christ, Amen.

When the song was finished, Matthew looked at his friend and smiled. He was the only one who heard him sing the song and enjoyed hearing them both sing the song in unison, one in German and the other in English. For the rest of the songs, Daniel just listened to the beautiful sounds. He missed this service and was glad Nathan had insisted they come.

The two-hour service went by quickly, and before they knew it, they were busy flipping the benches up to make tables, while the women went to the kitchen to put the meal out.

A group of young girls went to work setting bowls out for bean soup; filling glasses with water; and adding silverware, plates, and napkins to each spot. Meat, cheese, and bread, along with apple cinnamon moon pies, filled the tables.

Matthew took a seat at the end of the row next to Nathan.

"Did you catch Sarah up with what's going on in Willow Springs? The *kinner* couldn't stop talking about how much fun they had playing in the creek. Their heads barely hit the pillow last night, and they were out. I have to *denki* for wearing them out so much. It was nice they fell asleep early. My *mamm*'s been telling me Sarah was homesick, so you coming was perfect timing." He reached for a slice of bread as he said *denki* again.

"Those *kinner* of yours wore me out. I don't think I've slept that good in months. I should be thanking you," Matthew said.

"So, what do you think of the place?" Nathan asked.

"I'm amazed at how many horses you have. Not sure how you keep it all running so smooth but anxious to figure it out. I've been thinking about your offer to stay for a couple weeks. Does it still stand?"

"It sure does. I could use an extra pair of hands. We have a fence to fix, and ten more racehorses are being delivered next week. If your room in the loft is good, it sure would help me out."

Nathan held his cup up so one of the girls could come fill it with more water while he answered Matthew.

"Have you talked to your aunt this morning?" Nathan asked.

Matthew lifted his head and started to look around as he said, "She's here? I haven't seen her since I was little. I'm not sure I could pick her out among the women."

Nathan looked toward the women and said, "I don't see her at the moment, but after we're done eating, I'll help you find her."

"That would be great. I promised my *datt* I'd check on her, and I have a few gifts to give her. We passed Troyer Lane this morning, and I could see a farm from the road. Is that my cousin Martin's farm with the greenhouse out back?"

"It is. He built that greenhouse a few years ago and supplies the community with vegetables and flower plants every spring and fall. He's done well with his greenhouse business and doesn't do much farming anymore. He rents his barn to me every winter to store hay."

Nathan put the last bite of moon pie in his mouth and stood up.

"Let's go find them. I bet they're anxious to see you."

"I don't think they even know I'm here. I didn't have time to write and let them know I was coming. Daniel sprung this trip on me pretty quickly."

Matthew stood up and looked around the barn as he followed Nathan toward the back where the men were gathering. Nathan spotted Martin and walked his way.

"Martin, I have someone here that wants to see you."

With hearing his name, he turned around, just as Nathan and Matthew walked up behind him.

Matthew reached out his hand to Martin and said, "I'm sure you have no idea who I am, but I am Matthew, your cousin from Willow Springs."

"Well, what a surprise! What's brought you to Sugarcreek?"

"I tagged along with my friend, Daniel Miller, and promised my *datt* I would check on your *mamm* while I was here."

"Daniel Miller, well, that's a name I haven't heard in a while. I saw him this morning but haven't had a chance to say hello. I heard he moved to Willow Springs."

"Does my *mamm* know you are here? I'm sure she'll want to talk to you."

Matthew looked around the room as he said, "It's been so long since I've seen her. I don't remember what she looks like, not sure I could pick her out in a crowd if I wanted to."

"Well, let's go fix that," Martin said.

He followed Martin as he started to walk to the other side of the room. Once they got to the table where the older women were sitting, Martin waited until his *mamm* stopped talking before he tapped her on the shoulder.

When Anna Mae looked over her shoulder, she gasped at the sight of the two men. She couldn't take her eyes off Matthew.

"Oh my, you have to be Jacob's boy. You look just like him at that age."

"That I am," Matthew said with a smile on his face. He hadn't realized he looked so much like his *datt*, but by his aunt's reaction, he must.

She turned on the bench and said, "What has you so far from home?"

"It's a long story, but I promised *Datt* I would check on you and deliver a few gifts from my *mamm*. How about I let you finish your lunch and then we can visit? I'm staying at Nathan Bouteright's with my friend and can stop by and visit with you on my way back this afternoon."

"I'd love that," she said.

As Matthew turned to walk away, he noticed Sarah standing near the barn door all by herself.

He turned his attention to Martin and said, "Go ahead, I'll catch up with you in a minute. There's someone I need to talk to."

He walked toward Sarah, and when she saw him, she slipped outside and headed to the area where the buggies were lined up.

"Sarah, wait up," he hollered.

She knew he was following her and kept on walking, looking for a spot they could talk without being noticed. The last thing she wanted was for Nathan or Rosie to see them alone. The *kinner* were off playing, and Rosie was busy eating. At the moment, no one would miss her.

He followed her as she slipped behind a buggy. Once she was sure they couldn't be seen, she stopped and turned around. As she turned, he reached out and pulled her close. She leaned into him and laid her head on his chest but for only a moment.

She pushed him away, and with a smile on her face, she looked up at him.

"What was with squeezing my hand this morning? You startled me so much, I was sure the whole table felt me jump!"

"I just had to touch you."

She snuggled into his embrace again and said, "Oh, Matthew, what are we going to do?"

"Nathan needs a farmhand, and I need you, so I told him this morning I'm going to stay around for a few weeks. That'll give me some time to figure this all out. I already told you I'm not going to let you out of my sight again, if I can help it."

She pushed herself away again and started to ask him about his farm when he put his finger to her lips and pulled her back into his chest. He reached up and put his hand on the back of her head and gently tugged at the back of her *kapp*, pulling her head back so he could look into her eyes.

"I told you to stop worrying about this. We'll figure it out together."

As she looked into his eyes, she could see he was determined, and she needed to trust he'd figure out a way they could be together.

With a sense of longing, he pulled her even closer as he wrapped his arm around her waist. All at once, she knew he was in control and she would follow his lead, just as *Gott* had intended her to do.

Nathan looked at the table where the women sat eating and noticed Sarah was nowhere in sight. He smiled to himself, thinking she must be off tending to the *kinner*. She was so good to them, and they loved her so much. He couldn't imagine how they would have survived the past year without her. He knew he needed to send her back to Willow Springs and find a *fraa*. Lately, life was as normal as it could possibly be since Susan died, and he attributed that to Sarah. His mourning period had come to a close, and he was free to look for a *fraa*, but he just didn't think anyone could love his *kinner* more than Sarah did. With a content smile on his face, he turned his attention back to the conversation the men were having with Daniel.

Daniel stood in the middle of the group telling them all about his life in Willow Springs. It had been a couple years since he'd left Sugarcreek and had made several good friends among the community while working at the stables. He felt at home there and wished his father hadn't taken the job in Pittsburgh. In Willow Springs, he was considered an outsider and didn't fit in as well with the Amish community as he did in Sugarcreek. He had even been invited to attend the youth gathering that night. He looked around the barn for Matthew, and when he didn't see him, he figured he'd found some of his relatives and was visiting with them. He had to get serious about finding Elizabeth, but at the moment, he was enjoying visiting with his old friends.

Just as he was finishing up telling the story about Samuel Yoder being shot, he saw Matthew walk in through the open doors at the back of the barn. He could tell Matthew was looking past him and turned to see what had captured his attention. He saw Sarah walk through the doors at the front of the barn. He thought it was odd that they both walked through opposite doors at the very same time. By the look on both of their faces, he knew they had found a way to spend a few minutes alone. Matthew walked up beside Daniel and grabbed his shirt sleeve and pulled him away from the circle he was standing in.

"I spoke to my aunt, and I told her we would stop by this afternoon on our way back to Nathan's. I hope that's all right," he asked.

"Sure, when do you want to leave?"

"Let me go find my aunt and ask what time would be good," Matthew said.

Matthew left Daniel and walked to where the older women were sitting. The younger women were busy carrying dishes to the kitchen to be washed, and some of the men were stacking the benches inside the big church wagon parked in front of the barn. The older women were enjoying the shade the porch provided from the early afternoon sun.

Anna Mae saw him walking across the yard toward where she sat. Even the way he carried himself made her realize how much she missed her younger *bruder*. It had been too long since she'd seen Jacob and yearned to visit with him.

As he approached the porch, he heard her announce his arrival to those around her by stating that he was her nephew from Willow Springs, her *bruder* Jacob's oldest child.

"I just spoke to Daniel, and he was good with us stopping by on our way back to Nathan's this afternoon. I wanted to ask what time would be good for you."

"I was just thinking about finding Martin to ask him to take me home. He likes visiting, and it's hard for me to pull him away. If you and your friend are ready, would you mind just taking me home?"

"I know Daniel's anxious to get going. He has his own business to take care of today, and I'm sure he won't mind taking you home."

"That would be wonderful. I'll find Martin and let them know you'll be taking me home. Let me go gather the dishes I brought from the kitchen, and I'll meet you at the front of the house."

Anna Mae told her friends goodbye and set out to find her son.

Matthew turned and headed back to where he left Daniel when he spotted Sarah sitting in the grass under a maple tree, rocking Amos on her lap. Rachel sat on the ground next to her, playing with a few girls her age. Sarah looked at ease holding her nephew. She was kissing the top of his head while she was rocking him to sleep. He could see how much she cared for them and wasn't sure how he could convince her to leave them behind and move back to Willow Springs with him.

He hung his head as he walked back to the barn looking for Daniel. It wasn't hard to pull him away from his friends since he had made plans to attend the youth gathering that evening. Daniel waved goodbye and went to get the cart and horse from the paddock at the back of the barn.

Matthew walked out the barn doors and looked to his right to see if Sarah was still there. She was still sitting under the tree, holding Amos in her arms.

Just as he turned the corner, she looked up and saw him coming. She had to lower her head, so no one saw the smile on her face at seeing him walking her way. She laid Amos on the quilt on the ground next to her and stood up so she could talk to Matthew once he reached her.

Matthew was the first to speak, and he talked quietly so the *kinner* wouldn't stir too much.

"I am leaving to go visit my aunt before Daniel and I go look for his sister. I didn't want you to worry when I didn't go back to Nathan's right away."

"Thanks for letting me know. Nathan will be looking to gather us up to head home ourselves soon. He likes the *kinner* to take their naps at the same time every day. Amos started his early today, and it won't be long, and Rachel will be getting sleepy as well. Even Rosie likes to take a nap and will be asking Nathan to take her home soon. Sundays are the days Nathan and I sit on the porch and reminisce about Susan, and he looks forward to it each week."

There was something about the way Sarah describe sitting on the porch with Nathan that bothered him, but right now, he didn't have time to think about it. He could see his aunt waiting for him at the front of the house, and he needed to go.

"See you tonight," he said as he turned and walked away.

Sarah looked toward the barn and found Nathan looking her way. He was leaning up against the side of the barn door with his arms crossed. She'd never seen him look at her that way, and it suddenly made her uncomfortable. He must have been watching her as she talked to Matthew. She wondered if he could tell by watching them that she loved him. Concern changed the smile on her face to worry as she watched Nathan walk her way.

He didn't say a word as he scooped Amos off the ground and grabbed Rachel's hand to lead them to the buggy. All of a sudden, he was acting strange, and she felt uneasy walking behind him. Maybe it was her imagination, or maybe it was the guilt she felt from keeping Matthew a secret from him.

Chapter 16

Finding Elizabeth

It was a beautiful day for a ride in the open cart, and Anna Mae was enjoying the sun on her face.

"I can't remember the last time I rode in a cart. I'd forgotten how much I like it. *Denki* for taking me home and letting me feel like a teenager again."

All the way back to her house, she talked about the families that lived along the way. Most of them were cousins and relatives of Matthew's he'd never met. He couldn't believe he had so many relatives he didn't know. He silently thought he wanted to meet them all while he was in Sugarcreek.

As Daniel guided the cart to a stop at the end of Anna Mae's driveway, he had the uncanny feeling of déjà vu. He'd driven this road hundreds of times when he lived at Nathan's and never had that feeling before. He pulled the cart off to the side of the road to let a couple cars go by before he turned onto Troyer Lane. The horse became nervous when he pulled up close to the ditch and tried to pull the cart back to the center of the road.

Anna Mae mentioned that her late *mun* had pulled many a buggies and cars out of that ditch when they got too close and slid in. He looked beyond her and into the ditch. At that exact moment, he saw himself as a five-year-old huddled in a cold, wet ditch hiding from his father.

It took him a few minutes to look away and only after Matthew asked him if he was going to sit in the middle of the road all day. He slapped the reins to get the horse to turn down the driveway, but his thoughts were still in that ditch. He couldn't shake the feeling and remained quiet as they made their way to the end of the lane.

"Just pull up beside the *doddi haus* and let me off. I'll go get us something to drink while you go unhitch the cart."

Matthew looked around the farm at the main house that sat to the right of the *doddi haus* and the greenhouse behind the barn. It looked like his cousin had taken good care of his *doddi's* farm and was glad it stayed in the family. He didn't remember what it looked like since he was just a small boy the last time he visited.

Matthew hopped off the back of the cart and walked around front to help his aunt down. She gladly took his hand and again told him how much he reminded her of his *datt*.

Once he helped her down, he reached into the back of the cart for the bag that his *mamm* sent. Anna Mae waited for him, and they both walked up the steps of the front porch together.

"Take a seat here, and I'll be back in a minute."

Matthew took a seat and looked across the yard at Daniel who was still in the cart. He wondered why he was still sitting there, just staring down the driveway.

Daniel felt like he was in a trance. Memories were flooding in from all directions. He could hear his father's angry screams, police sirens, and a baby crying. He could swear he was having a nightmare in the middle of the day. He shook his head, trying to push the memories away. He couldn't imagine what had brought them on all at once.

He looked over at Matthew and back down the driveway. *What is it with that ditch that ignited those painful memories?*

He ran his hand through his hair and jumped off the cart, trying to force the negative feelings to go away. As he tied the cart to the post, he looked back down Troyer Lane. He'd never driven down the lane before, even though he'd passed it many times. There was something about that ditch that scared him.

He stood looking up the lane with his back to the porch. He closed his eyes, trying to clear his head, when the memories came again.

It was cold and dark in the ditch, and he could feel the mud between his toes. He'd taken his shoes off in the back of the car and didn't have time to grab them when his mother unfastened his seat belt and told him to run and hide in the ditch. He remembered digging his feet in the mud, trying to keep his mind off the baby crying.

He wanted to go get his sister and comfort her, but his mother had told him not to make a sound and to stay hidden in the ditch, no matter what. He could hear his father screaming for the baby to shut up over his mother begging him to stop. All of a sudden, he heard a strange noise and was listening carefully, trying to figure out what it was.

His father had stopped hollering, and all he heard was a sound he couldn't place.

That was sixteen years ago, why do I remember it so vividly right now? he thought.

Still standing in the middle of the driveway, he opened his eyes to see Martin and his family coming down the lane in their buggy. In his nightmares, he'd always heard the same noise, and then it hit him. The sound he heard was the clip-clop of a horse and buggy.

Martin pulled his buggy up to the main house to let his family off and then drove it around the circle driveway where Daniel was standing.

"Are you staying long? You can unhitch your horse and bring her into the barn for some grain and water if you want," Martin said.

"I don't think we will be staying long. She'll be good right here, if it's okay?"

"Looks good to me. Let me put this buggy away, and I'll come sit with you on the porch. I want to get to know my cousin better."

The short conversation with Martin forced the memories away for a few minutes as he turned and made his way to the porch. He pulled up a chair and sat down right next to Matthew.

"Are you okay? You look like you've seen a ghost."

Daniel looked back toward the road and just shook his head, trying to shake it off.

"There's something about that ditch that brought back a bunch of crazy memories. I think all this talk about finding Elizabeth is bringing up a bunch of things I've tried hard to forget. I just want to get all this business taken care of and get back to Willow Springs."

Just then, Anna Mae opened the screen door carrying a tray of glasses and a pitcher of tea.

"I'm so happy you boys decided to come and visit with me. I want to hear all about your life in Willow Springs. It's been years since I've seen my *bruder* and his family, I want to hear everything."

With a happy spring in her step, she poured the tea and sat down ready to listen.

Just then, Martin stepped up on the porch and took a seat on the railing.

"So, tell me, cousin, what brings you to Sugarcreek?"

"It's Daniel that brought me here. He's on a mission to find his long-lost sister, and I needed a change of scenery, so I rode along."

He wasn't sure how much Daniel wanted to say, so he turned to him as if asking him to continue.

"Now that's an interesting tale. How do you lose a sister?"

Looking a bit forlorn, Daniel answered, "It's a long story, but the short of it is, we were separated when we were little. I was placed in a foster home, and I'm not sure whatever happened to her."

"So how do you find someone if you have no idea what happened to her?" Anna Mae asked.

"I have an address where she was seen last, so that's where I'm going to start. I'm not even sure I'll get anywhere, but I promised my mother I'd at least try."

He was glad Anna Mae was excited to hear all about Matthew's family and quickly turned the conversation around by asking Matthew about his sisters.

With a questioning look, Anna Mae turned toward Matthew and asked, "How old are your *schwesters* now?"

"Let's see, Rebecca and Anna are almost eighteen, and Emma turns sixteen today."

All of a sudden, Anna Mae turned her head and looked up the lane as if she remembered something painful. The look on her face changed, and everyone noticed.

"What is it, *Mamm*?" Martin asked.

"I'd forgotten this is the week sixteen years ago your *doddi* died. That was the last time I'd seen my *bruder* face to face. They hired a car to bring them to the funeral. Your *mamm* was pregnant at the time and went into labor the day before we buried my *datt*."

"Was Emma born here?" Matthew asked.

It was a few minutes before she answered. "Yes, she was born in Sugarcreek."

Martin continued to ask Matthew about his family and his work on the farm, while both Anna Mae and Daniel sat in silence.

Daniel was consumed with the flood of memories that attacked him, while Anna Mae was lost in her own thoughts as she remembered that horrible night sixteen years ago.

She knew she'd have to relive that night at some point, but thought it would be when Marie Cooper showed up on her doorstep, not her nephew. Just thinking about that night made her want to go lay down.

"This old lady needs a nap, so if you men don't mind, I'm gonna go lie down." She didn't even wait for an answer before she stood up and went into the house.

Matthew looked at Martin and asked him if his *mamm* was all right.

"She often gets that faraway look in her eyes, but normally, it's when someone mentions my *datt*'s name. This is the first time I've seen it when she talked about her own *datt*. It's been an exciting day with your visit, so I'm sure she just needs to rest."

Martin jumped off the railing, grabbed his hat, and headed for the steps.

"I'd better go see what my family's up to. Those *kinner* are a handful. I'm sure my *fraa* would like some help. It was nice to visit with you. Stop by again before you leave. I'm sure my family would like to meet you."

Matthew stood up and looked at Daniel as he asked, "Are you ready to go find your sister?"

Daniel nodded his head and followed Matthew off the porch.

As Daniel climbed in the cart, Matthew unhitched the horse from the post and climbed up. Daniel slapped the reins and started down the driveway.

"Let's go trade this horse in for my truck and get this over with. I have the address in my wallet. I'll dig it out in a minute. Who knows? It might be close, and I won't need to get my truck."

As he approached the end of the lane, he pulled off beside the mailbox. He handed Matthew the reins while he shifted to one side to retrieve his wallet from his back pocket. It took him a few minutes to find the small piece of paper he'd torn from his mother's letter. When he opened it, he read the address out loud.

"1042 Troyer Lane, Sugarcreek, Ohio."

Daniel looked at Matthew as he pointed to the mailbox. Handpainted in black letters on the white mailbox was written "1042 Troyer Lane."

He crumbled the paper in his hands and pushed it into his pocket as he had grabbed the reins from Matthew. He guided the horse out into the middle of the road to turn around to head back to Martin's Farm.

They didn't say a word as he pulled the cart up in front of the *doddi haus*. He handed the reins to Matthew as he jumped down from his seat and ran up the stairs. He knocked on the door, and as he waited for Anna Mae to answer, he turned to Matthew and said, "You'd better unhitch the horse this time. I think we'll be here a while."

Matthew was in shock and couldn't believe the answers Daniel came looking for might be coming from his family. He led the horse away and into the barn.

Daniel stood on the porch, trying to gather his thoughts, while he waited for Anna Mae to answer the door. He hoped she hadn't gone to lie down yet. He knew she was tired, but he had to find out what she might know about Elizabeth.

The window on the porch was open, and he could hear her feet shuffle against the hardwood floors. When she opened the door, she was surprised to see him standing in front of her.

"Daniel, did you forget something?"

He wasn't sure what to say, so he handed her the piece of paper with her address written on it.

"I'm sorry to bother you, I know you wanted to take a nap, but I think you might know where my sister is."

"I'm not sure I understand," she said.

"My mother is Marie Cooper."

Anna Mae covered her mouth with her hand and pushed the door opened so he could follow her inside.

"Come in. We have lots to talk about."

Matthew finished making the horse comfortable and returned to the house. The front door was wide open, so he walked in, shut the door, and followed their voices to the kitchen.

Anna Mae was at the sink, filling a tea kettle, as Daniel sat at the table, tapping his fingers on the table.

Matthew looked at Daniel as he turned his hands over and shrugged his shoulder as if to ask, *Well, what did she say?*

Daniel mouthed the words "Nothing yet."

Anna Mae didn't know where to start, so she busied herself with making tea and laying out a plate of cookies. All these years, she feared Marie Cooper would show up on her doorstep demanding to know what happened to her daughter, not her son.

Matthew couldn't stand it any longer and spoke up.

"Aunt Anna Mae, why would Daniel's mother give him your address to find his sister?"

With tears in her eyes, she pulled out a chair and sat down.

"Because I know where she is."

Two hours later, Matthew and Daniel climbed back into the cart for the ride to Nathan's. They both were in shock at what Anna Mae had described.

Matthew was the first to speak.

"This is not going to go over well, once we get back home. I can't believe my parents kept this from us for all these years. What's the bishop going to do once he finds out?"

With a sharpness in his voice, Daniel answered, "It's not like they planned it. I'm sure they did what they felt was best at the moment. My mother put them on the spot, and for the way I see it, my mom was in the wrong. How could she ask a complete stranger to hide her child? Whether it's right or wrong, all I know is, it kept Elizabeth from being placed in a foster home. For that, I'm grateful."

Matthew was angry and confused. His parents had been living a lie for sixteen years, and he felt betrayed.

They continued their ride in silence. Matthew was concerned at how this news was going to affect his family and his plans to remain in Sugarcreek. Daniel, on the other hand, had mixed emotions. He was relieved that he had found the answers he was looking for and felt anticipation at seeing Elizabeth.

All this time, she'd been right under my nose, he thought, *and I didn't know it. How is she going to react when she finds out who her brother is?*

Daniel pulled the cart up beside the stable and jumped down as he said, "I think we should pack up and head home right away."

"Okay, but I need to talk to Sarah first. The last she knew, I was staying in Sugarcreek. She'll be disappointed I'm leaving."

"I'll go find Nathan and tell him we're leaving while you go look for Sarah and explain things to her."

He helped Daniel unhitch the cart and rub Ester down before he put her back out to pasture. They both went up to the loft to pack their bags before they went to talk to Nathan and Sarah. It didn't take long, and they both were walking out the stable doors together. Daniel headed to the house while Matthew turned right to see if Sarah was at the *doddi haus*.

Sarah had seen them pull in the driveway and was sitting by the front window reading when Matthew came up on the porch. The *kinner* were with Nathan, so she was all alone. She had opened the door before he had a chance to knock.

With a big smile, she greeted him with a warm hello. With one look, she knew something was terribly wrong.

"We need to talk."

She placed her hand on his arm and said, "I think we'd better stay out on the porch where we can be seen. Nathan and Rosie won't approve of us being in the *haus* alone."

He turned on his heel and went and sat down in the rocker closest to the door.

Sarah followed him and sat in the chair next to him.

"What's the matter? You look so serious. Have you changed your mind about staying?"

"I can't explain everything right now or at least until I talk to my family, but we're leaving in a few minutes to go home. I know I told you I was staying, but something has come up that I must go take care of at home."

He took a look at the main house before he placed his hand over hers. He gave her hand a gentle squeeze and continued, "As soon as I've had a chance to talk to my *datt*, I'll be back. There's plenty of time before my fields need to be harvested to come back and help Nathan, so please don't worry."

Tears started to form in the corners of her eyes. She was so happy this morning when he held her; she felt like there was finally hope they could be together. Now she was worried it wouldn't happen after all.

"Please don't cry. I promise I'll be back" was all he said.

It was hard seeing the disappointment on her face. He should've explained what was going on, but he didn't have time. He saw Daniel pull the truck up close to the porch and, in a bold move, leaned in and kissed her forehead.

At that point, she didn't care who saw them; she was sure Daniel's truck was blocking their view from the main house. She reached up and laid her hand on the side of his face and said, "Please hurry back."

After they pulled away, she sat on the porch for the longest time, trying to figure out what was so important that they needed to leave so quickly. Matthew had never broken a promise before, so she trusted that he'd be back to her soon.

Nathan stood in the living room, looking out the window at Sarah sitting on her porch. He saw Matthew kiss her forehead and saw her tenderly touch his face. He didn't understand why she was keeping it a secret that Matthew was in love with her. Furthermore, why was he bothered about it? Was it because he loved her too?

Chapter 17

Emma's Birthday

Emma woke to the sound of a rooster crowing and a warm breeze coming through her window. She stretched and smiled as she remembered it was her birthday. She'd waited so long for this day; nothing was going to spoil it. She kicked off her blankets and sat on the edge of the bed.

Last night, her *datt* reminded her again that he wanted to talk to her after church. She couldn't help but feel nervous, but was determined not to dwell on it. The seriousness in his voice made her believe he had something important to discuss. She hoped he was finally going to tell her what he meant by her life was never going to be the same. For weeks, that was all she could think of. On a couple of occasions, she tried to ask her *mamm* what he meant, but she always brushed her off and told her they would explain everything soon. She pushed it all out of her mind and started to think of Samuel.

She hadn't seen him for weeks and was excited to see him at church that morning. Ever since he came home from the hospital, he'd stayed close to home, working with his physical therapist and getting stronger. Every time she'd seen Katie, she gave her an update on his progress. She'd feel better when she could see him in person.

She sat on the edge of her bed longer than usual and could tell by the smells that were drifting up the stairs that her *mamm* had already started breakfast. It was a tradition in her family that a birthday meant you got excused from chores for the whole day. Even though it was Sunday and no chores were done, she did get out of feeding the chickens and gathering eggs. This meant she could take her time getting out of bed. She was so excited she could hardly stand it.

She reached for her brush on the nightstand as she pulled her hair over her shoulder. She looked down at the blonde strands as she brushed out the tangles. She always thought it was strange she was the only one in her family with blonde hair and brown eyes. When she was little, she'd asked her *mamm* about it. At the time, she was told *Gott* blessed her by spraying her hair with sunshine before she was born. When she was five, she giggled at the thought of it and went on with her day. But today, she had the uncanny feeling it mattered.

She finished brushing her hair and rolled it tightly in a bun at the nape of her neck and secured her *kapp* with straight pins. She walked to the peg on the wall and grabbed her best blue dress and white apron. Once she made her bed and finished dressing, she started down the stairs, with Someday following close behind her. Her *mamm* never liked the dog in the house, but it was determined to follow her everywhere she went, no matter how much her *mamm* complained about it.

Someday was still a big mystery to her. She'd never found out who left him in a picnic basket on their back porch. She reached down and petted the top of his head as she remembered the day she found him.

Valentine's Day two years earlier

Emma rolled over in bed and pulled the blankets up over her head as she heard her mamm call her name from the bottom of the stairs. She hated the long winter months and dreaded walking to school in the cold. She was looking forward to the warmer months and wished she could stay in bed longer.

"Emma, you'll be late for school, if you don't get up right this minute," her *mamm* called.

With hearing the sharpness in her voice, she knew she needed to face the cold and get out of bed. She peeked her head out from underneath the warmth of her favorite quilt as she looked at the windup clock on the nightstand. It was six o'clock.

With a deep sigh, she threw the blankets off and swung her feet over the edge of the bed. The floor was cold, and she shivered as she looked for her stockings. She quickly put them on to ward off the chill and walked to the window. The window was frosty on the inside, and she used the warmth of her hand to melt a spot so she could look out. It was still dark, and she knew by the clear sky it would be a cold walk to school.

She heard her *mamm* call again, and she answered that she was up and would be down in a minute. She left the window and changed from her nightgown into her dress and apron, made her bed, and headed downstairs.

As she reached the last step, she heard her *schwesters*, Rebecca and Anna, cheerfully talking about their plans for the day. By the wonderful smells coming from the kitchen, she knew they had already started the cookies she'd planned to take to school with her.

"Well, good morning, sleepyhead," Rebecca said with a sense of sarcasm in her voice.

She knew better than to feed into her *schwester*'s snippy comment, so she walked over and hugged her as she thanked her for starting the cookies.

It was Valentine's Day, and she wanted to take in a treat to share with her class. Katie loved her Melt-in-Your-Mouth Sugar Cookies and decided that it was what she'd bake. They were best right out of the oven, so she wanted to wait until the morning to bake them. As she took the spoon and bowl from Rebecca, she told her *mamm* that as soon as she got this last pan of cookies in the oven, she'd go feed the chickens.

Her *mamm* smiled and told her to bundle up before she went outside. Emma pulled her coat from the peg in the mudroom and grabbed the egg basket as she headed out the door. She pulled her brown bonnet over her eyes and walked to the henhouse from memory. The winter wind was cold, and it was stinging her eyes as she walked. She reached for the door to the henhouse and noticed someone had tied a yellow ribbon on the door handle. It had snow on it and looked like it had been tied there for a while. She couldn't imagine who would have done such a thing. She untied the ribbon and opened the door, she put it in her pocket to show her *mamm* when she went inside.

It was cold, and she didn't waste any time gathering eggs, breaking the ice from the water and adding chicken scratch to the feeders. As she walked back to the house, she noticed footprints in the snow. By the look of the footprints, they were from whoever tied the door shut with the ribbon.

Once she returned to the house, her *mamm* had her lunch box packed and placed the freshly baked cookies on top so they wouldn't get crushed on the walk to school. She didn't have a chance to tell her about the ribbon before she rushed out the door for her thirty-minute walk.

As she turned left at the end of her driveway, she put her hand in her pocket and pulled out the yellow ribbon. She hadn't noticed before, but there was writing on it. It looked like someone had taken a black sharpie and written words on one strand of the ribbon.

She stopped alongside the road and placed her lunch box down and pulled the ribbon straight out with two hands so she could read what was written. In perfect penmanship were the words, "It's too soon." She shook her head trying to make sense of the phrase and couldn't imagine what it meant. She put it back in her pocket, picked up her lunch box, and started walking faster toward Katie's house.

As she crested the small hill, she saw Katie waiting at the end of her driveway.

"What took you so long? I didn't think you'd ever get here. It's cold, and I just want to get to school and warm up."

As they walked side by side, Emma told her about making her favorite cookies and about the yellow ribbon she'd found. They both tried to figure out what the words meant and who would do such a thing.

They were almost to school when Emma stopped and asked, "Where's Samuel?"

He always walked them to school in the winter on his way to work at the lumber mill. Emma was so caught up with the yellow ribbon, she didn't even think to ask about him earlier.

Katie shook her head and shrugged her shoulders as she said, "He was up and out the door before sunrise. He said he had something to take care of and wouldn't be able to walk us to school today."

As they walked through the schoolhouse doors, they noticed everyone was already in their seats. They hung up their coats and sat at their desks. As the teacher started to recite their morning scripture verse, Emma opened the top of her desk to retrieve her pad and pencil.

She couldn't believe her eyes—someone had placed a bag of chocolate kisses, tied with the same yellow ribbon in the top of her desk. She looked around the room to see if anyone was looking her way, and when she noticed no one was paying any mind to her, she quietly pulled the bag out and placed it on her lap. Keeping one eye on the teacher and one eye on the bag of chocolates, she untied the ribbon and stretched it on her lap so she could read the message written on it.

In the same perfect penmanship were written the words, "But someday."

Emma was more confused than ever and couldn't wait until lunch so she could talk to Katie. At lunch, the girls sat in the corner of the room comparing the ribbons as they ate their meal.

"What could it mean?" Katie asked.

"I just don't know. I keep looking around the room trying to see if anyone is staring at me, but nothing. There has to be a meaning to it all, but it beats me to figure it out."

Just then, the teacher asked everyone to finish up and take their seats. For now, the mystery of the chocolate kisses and the yellow ribbons would have to wait.

With both of the ribbons tucked away in her lunchbox, she took her seat and concentrated on her schoolwork. Toward the end of the day, the teacher gave them permission to pass out their Valentine's Day treats and exchange cards with the other students.

As each of them compared their cards and enjoyed their cookies, the teacher told them she was dismissing them early so they could go home and play before it got dark. The whole class erupted in a loud cheer as they gathered up their treats and raced to the back of the room to put on their coats and head home.

When Emma got home, she noticed her *datt*'s buggy was gone and her *mamm* and *schwesters* were nowhere to be found. There was a note on the kitchen table telling her they'd gone to the Mercantile and would be back shortly. She was instructed to peel potatoes for supper and set the table.

As she started to set the table, she hoped her *datt* was in the furniture shop so she could ask permission to go skating. Just as she was about to go down to the basement for potatoes, she heard a strange noise coming from the mudroom.

When she opened the door, there sat a big wicker picnic basket with a pretty yellow ribbon tied to the handle. The noise she was hearing was coming from inside the basket. She knelt down and carefully peeked inside. As she opened the lid, a chocolate lab puppy came barreling out and jumped into her lap.

She fell backward, and the puppy was covering her face with kisses. She wrapped her arms around the dog and sat upright, holding the puppy close. Right away, she noticed it had a collar on, and dangling from the collar was a tag with the name "SOMEDAY" imprinted on it. The yellow ribbon and the bag of chocolate kisses had been leading up to this Valentine's Day surprise, she was sure of it. But who could have given her such a gift?

She crossed her legs and let the puppy sit on her lap as she smiled at the events of the day. For a day that had started out cold and dreary, it sure was ending up full of mystery and excitement.

That was two years ago, and she still had no idea who gave her the special gift.

As she walked into the kitchen, she saw her birthday cake sitting in the middle of the table, with a gift sitting at her spot. Her parents were both sitting at the table sipping their coffee and looked up and wished her a happy birthday as she came into the room.

She smiled and pulled out her chair and sat down.

"Can you believe I'm sixteen?"

"Believe me, we can't either," her *mamm* said.

She looked at her *datt*, and as usual, he didn't say a word as he went back to reading *The Budget*. When he was done, he set his paper down and said, "We'll be coming home right after church today, and we've asked your *schwesters* to stay at the Yoder's for the afternoon. We'll be walking and not taking the buggy."

Trying to lighten the mood her *mamm* said, "Why don't you go ahead and open your present now."

Emma smiled as she picked up the gift wrapped in simple brown paper and tied with a thin pink ribbon. She carefully untied it and took the brown paper off the box. Inside were four pretty pink glass dessert plates.

It was a custom in her *g'may* that a young girl pick a favorite color when they were five years old, and she'd picked pink. Choosing a color when they were young meant that they had years of receiving gifts in their color to add to their hope chest. By the time a young girl married, she had many useful household items to set up a home. The four plates would complete a full set of twelve she had already stored in her chest at the foot of her bed.

She couldn't think of a more perfect gift. She thanked her parents and looked at the cake in the middle of the table.

"Did Anna make the cake?" she asked.

All three girls had things that they were good at. Emma loved to garden, Rebecca was good at spinning, and Anna could bake. On some occasions, her baked goods were even better than her *mamm*'s, and that was saying a lot since her *mamm* baked bread for the Haven Sandwich Shop.

She reached up and took a taste of the buttercream frosting just as her *schwesters* came in the side door.

"It seems strange without Matthew here," Rebecca said as she pulled her chair out and sat to the left of her *datt*.

Once both girls sat down, Stella stood up and retrieved the egg-and sausage casserole that had been cooling on the top of the stove.

Jacob bowed his head in prayer and silently asked the Lord to give him the words to help Emma deal with all they needed to share with her that afternoon.

It wasn't long, and they were walking to the Yoder's for church.

Once they got there, Stella and the girls walked in the side door, straight into Ruth's kitchen. Stella warmly kissed Ruth on the cheek and asked her how Samuel was feeling. Ruth smiled as she described he'd been in a good mood that morning.

With hearing that, Emma smiled and quickly walked through the kitchen and into the front room where the benches had already been set up for service. The older women were filling in and taking their places. They only had church every other Sunday, and it was like clockwork how they all came in the exact same way each time. Not only did they file in the same way, but they also all took the exact same spots on the benches.

When it was her turn to come in and sit down, she reached down and picked up the *Aushund* that sat in her spot and placed it on her lap as she sat. She folded her hands on top of the book and waited for the rest of members to take their seats. Their district was getting bigger, and soon it would split in two. Most Sundays, all the benches on the men's side filled up, which left the boys standing up against the wall. Samuel and some of the other men were letting the younger boys sit while they leaned on the wall.

She noticed his arm was still in a sling, and he had a warm smile back on his face. Her heart melted when she saw him and was pleased he looked better. That night's *singeon* couldn't get there fast enough, and hopefully, he'd ask to take her home.

When the song leader started to sing the first song, Emma picked up her book and turned to page 744. She didn't know all the words and was anxious to find it so she could sing along. When she opened the book, she saw a glimpse of something yellow peeking out from above the pages.

With excitement, she turned to where the yellow ribbon was marking the spot. Lying neatly between the pages was the same yellow ribbon she had received two years earlier when Someday showed up in the mudroom. Written in the same perfect penmanship were the words, "It's time."

She didn't dare look up from her songbook for fear someone would notice how flush she was. With her head bent down, as if she was singing from the book, she closed her eyes and tried to make sense of this third message. It had been two years since the last message, and she was trying to remember what the others had said. The first message was "It's too soon"; the second message was, "But someday"; and then this third message, "It's time."

Time for what? she thought.

Her heart was racing as she continued to keep her eyes closed. She let the sound of the cappella music fill her ears. She could hear the slow song being sung and tried to let the harmonic tune calm her excitement over the ribbon.

Only when the song was over did she dare look up. From across the room, she could feel someone looking at her, and she hoped it was Samuel. The vorsinger started to sing the second song, and she fell into unison with the girls around her as they sang the "Lob Lied."

Samuel was so nervous that the songbooks would get mixed up when the girls sat down that he was relieved when he saw the yellow ribbon dangling from the book Emma held close to her chest. When he looked at her, she had a peaceful smile on her face, and he smiled back.

She looked deep into Samuel's eyes, and it finally hit her who had given her Someday and who the yellow ribbon messages had been from. She was sure by the look on his face that the messages came from him, and he would surely explain everything to her that night.

As soon as the service was over and the men started to convert the benches into tables, Jacob found Stella and told her they would not be staying for the meal. He wanted her to find Emma so they could head home. He told her he was too nervous to eat and felt it was better to leave right away.

Emma slipped out the side door and was standing near the corner of the house talking to Katie when Stella found her.

"There you are. Your *datt* is ready to go. We won't be staying for lunch. Please say your goodbyes and meet us out front."

"Without eating?" Emma asked.

"Yes, please, no arguing. Just do as I say."

Emma was disappointed; she had hoped to get a chance to talk to Samuel and ask him about the ribbons. She knew better that to argue with her *mamm* and went ahead and told her friends goodbye before heading around to the front of the house. Just as she rounded the corner, she bumped smack into Samuel.

"There you are, I was looking for you," he said.

He quickly looked around to see if anyone was watching them and said, "I've been waiting for this day forever. I have so much to tell you. Please tell me you will be at the *singeon* tonight?"

"I'll be there, and I'm expecting an explanation about this ribbon. I don't have time to talk right now. My parents are waiting for me, but you'll have my complete attention tonight."

With a smile on her face, she slipped past him to meet her parents.

As Emma came up to her parents, she noticed her *mamm* had a worried look on her face and was leaning into her *datt*, whispering. As soon as they saw her, they turned and walked toward the road. She fell into step behind them and could feel a heaviness in the air. She didn't understand what was so important that it couldn't wait until they had at least eaten lunch. She could tell by the way her *datt* was walking it wasn't a good time for her to question him. It was a short walk back to the farm, and as soon as they got to the steps of the porch, he stopped and turned to speak to her.

"You go in the house with your *mamm*, and I'll be right in," he turned and walked toward the furniture shop.

As she looked at her *mamm,* she asked, "You're both making me nervous. What could be so important that we had to leave without eating lunch?"

Stella reached out and took her hand and directed her up the stairs and into the house. Once they got to the kitchen, she told her to sit down, and she'd make her a sandwich as they waited for her *datt* to come back.

Emma felt a sense of gloom fall over the room, and she couldn't shake the feeling that whatever they needed to talk to her about was serious. She knew it was the day for explanations. She finally figured out the secret behind the yellow ribbons, and now she was about to discover the secret her parents had been keeping from her.

Stella busied herself making sandwiches and pouring glasses of tea, as she waited for Jacob to return. She knew what he had gone to the furniture shop for and was not looking forward to explaining everything to Emma.

As Jacob came back into the house, he carried a small wooden box and sat it on the table in front of Emma. He placed his hand on the box and said, "Before you look in this box, we have something we want to share with you. The contents of this box will explain a lot, but we want you to know that we only did what we felt was needed to keep you safe, and we don't regret any of the decisions we've made. We couldn't be prouder of you and hope that after this day, you'll continue to think of us as your parents. We made a promise sixteen years ago that on your sixteen birthday we would tell you about your family."

Jacob pulled out his chair and sat at the table as he motioned for Stella to do the same. Once they both were seated, he nodded his head, giving Emma permission to open the wooden box.

She felt scared, and her head was spinning, trying to make sense of everything he had said. *What did he mean by saying he hoped I'd always think of them as my parents? What other family do I have?*

She opened the lid and looked in the box. The contents confused her as she pulled each item out. The first thing she retrieved was a torn and tattered picture of a little boy holding a *boppli*. On the back of the picture, names were written in blue ink, "Daniel, 5, and Elizabeth, 1 week."

She couldn't help but have an eerie feeling when she looked in the eyes of the little boy. She laid the photo down and reached back into the box and pulled out a stack of letters all addressed to someone named Elizabeth Cooper at 1042 Troyer Lane, Sugarcreek, Ohio, and all had been postmarked in July for the last fifteen years.

She laid the stack of letters down and picked up the newspaper clipping of a woman. The picture showed a woman with blonde hair and brown eyes holding a police booking card. The story caption read, "Sugarcreek Woman Sentenced to 20 years for Voluntary Manslaughter."

The last items were a birth certificate for Elizabeth Marie Cooper and a small pink blanket with the initials EMC embroidered in the corner. She picked up the photo and looked long and hard at the little boy in the picture again. There was something so familiar about him, almost like she'd seen those eyes before. The boy had blonde hair and brown eyes. Then it hit her. She was the *boppli* in the picture.

She looked at her *mamm* and choked on a sob that was lodged in her throat. A sense of sadness filled the air so much that it suffocated her. She couldn't look at another thing. She pushed the box off the table and ran out of the house.

Stella jumped up to stop her, but Jacob grabbed her arm and told her to let her go.

"We have to explain, she has to know what happened, and we can't just let her run off," Stella cried.

"She'll be back. Let her absorb what she's figured out so far. Once she has, she'll be back, and we can tell her more."

Chapter 18

The Secret

Emma ran out, letting the screen door slam as she passed through. She stood on the front porch only for a second before heading down the steps and straight to the barn. All she could think of was getting as far away from her parents as she could. Once in the barn, she climbed the hayloft stairs and went to the hidden cubby hole she used whenever she wanted to be alone. The smell of hay and the stillness of the empty barn gave her comfort.

She was still shaking, trying to make sense of it all. She felt as if her life was a lie. She wasn't Emma Byler, daughter of Jacob and Stella, but Elizabeth Cooper, the daughter of a woman convicted of manslaughter. She didn't even know what *manslaughter* meant, but it didn't sound good. In her hand, she still held the photo of the little boy and flipped it over to read the names again. Daniel was clearly written on the back along with her name, Elizabeth.

Who is he, but more importantly, is he my bruder, *and where is he now? Nothing makes sense*, she thought.

She reached between the rafters and pulled out a box she'd kept hidden there. She hadn't looked at the box in years and was surprised to find her favorite doll inside. She sat on the straw-covered floor and curled up in a ball. She pulled the doll tight to her chest and let the sobs release from her throat.

Stella couldn't sit still. She was pacing from window to window, praying Emma was okay. She heard the chime on the clock ring three times, telling her it had been close to two hours since she'd run from the house.

"We have to find her. She didn't even give us time to explain. Oh, Jacob, I'm so worried, would you please go look for her?"

"You stay here, in case she comes back, and I'll go look for her."

Thirty minutes later, as she was in the kitchen making a cup of tea, she heard the screen door slam and ran to the front room hoping it was Emma.

"I've looked everywhere, and she's nowhere to be found. I even walked down to the creek and nothing. I'm sure once she's had time to calm down, she'll come back looking for answers."

Emma opened her eyes at the sound of her *datt* calling her name. She'd fallen asleep, and it took her a minute to remember where she was. Her head was pounding, and the ribbons of her *kapp* were soaked with tears. She had no idea how long she'd been asleep.

By the position of the sun that seeped through the cracks in the barn wall, she figured it must be midafternoon. She stood up and brushed the straw off her dress. The doll and the photo lay at her feet. She reached down to put the doll back in the box and glanced at the picture. All of a sudden, she realized where she'd seen those eyes. They were the same color as hers, and they belonged to Daniel Miller.

She picked up the picture. It had to be him. How was she going to tell him the sister he went looking for was right under his nose? Her head was spinning, and before she could do anything else, she needed to talk to her parents. Just the thought of hearing the truth made her sick, but it was time to hear the whole story.

Jacob and Stella were sitting on the front porch when Emma came out of the barn. Stella laid her hand on Jacob's arm.

"Oh, thank goodness. There she is."

Emma stood looking at them, trying not to cry. Her feet wouldn't move, no matter how hard she tried. All she kept hearing were her *datt*'s words, *"Her life will never be the same."* She didn't want her life to change; she liked things just the way they were.

When she saw him stand up and walk off the porch toward her, the tears started to fall again. How could this be happening? The man walking toward her was the only *datt* she'd ever known. Who and where was her real *datt*?

From the little bit she'd read from the newspaper clipping, she figured out her mother was in prison, but she didn't see anything about her *datt*. She was desperately trying to fit all the pieces together.

When Jacob made it close enough that he could reach her, he pulled her into his arms. Over the past six months, he'd barely talked to her, and when he did it was in harsh tones and an overprotectiveness she didn't understand. His tender embrace made her collapse in his arms.

"I don't understand. Please tell me you're my *datt* and this is just some big mistake. I don't want to be Elizabeth—I want to be Emma."

By then, the sobs were shaking her body; and with one swoop, he picked her up, cradled her in his arms, and carried her to the house. Stella moved to open the screen door as he walked past. He laid her down on the sofa and told Stella he was going to go get her a drink and a cold rag for her face.

Stella sat on the edge of the couch and wiped Emma's tears with the corner of her apron.

"You need to let us explain. Things will make sense when you've heard the whole story."

Emma reached into her pocket and pulled out the photo.

"I need to talk to Daniel."

"Daniel, in the picture? We have no idea where to find him."

"I do," she said as she pulled herself up on the couch.

Just then, her *datt* came back into the room, carrying a glass of water and a cold washcloth for her face.

"Please take a drink, wipe your face, and calm down so we can talk to you."

Emma took the washcloth, opened it, and laid her face in it to help ease her swollen eyes.

Stella looked up at Jacob and whispered, "She says she knows where to find Daniel."

She pulled the washcloth away from her face and looked at her *datt*.

"It's Daniel Miller."

"Daniel? Matthew's friend?"

"Why would you think that?"

"Before they left for Sugarcreek, Daniel told me that he was going there to look for his sister and that his mother was in prison. The letters in the box all had a Sugarcreek address on them and the woman in the picture is in prison. Look at the picture—that's Daniel, I'm sure of it."

Stella took the photo from her and walked over to the light of the window so she could see it better. The photo was old and tattered, but when she looked at it again, she could see the resemblance to Daniel Miller.

"Jacob, I think she might be right. This boy does look like him. Did Matthew tell you why they were going to Ohio?"

"No, he just said he was going along for the ride while Daniel took care of some business for his mother. I assumed he meant 'Mrs. Miller.'"

Jacob sat down in the chair by the window, still holding the photo that Stella had handed him. She went back to the sofa and sat down beside Emma. She took her hand and picked Emma's chin up with one finger, so she could look in her eyes.

"Emma, you're our daughter, no matter what a piece of paper says. We love you, and that will never change. Whether your *bruder* is Daniel Miller or not, time will only tell, but we do know where your mother is, and that she wants to be a part of your life. We made a promise sixteen years ago, and we intend to keep it. Before your *datt* tells you what happened, you have to understand that we kept this secret from you because we wanted you to be old enough to understand the choices you need to make."

"What are you talking about? The only choice I've been given is the choice not to be Emma Byler."

"Now just let your *datt* explain."

She looked his way waiting for him to start talking. He sat in his chair, trying to force himself to relive the day when he first saw her.

Jacob looked up at Emma and knew he couldn't keep the ugliness of the outside world from her any longer. In the last six months, he'd forbidden Emma to leave his sight for fear Marie Cooper would find her. He'd hidden the truth about her abusive father, the unfair prison term her mother was serving, and a *bruder* she knew nothing about.

In a selfless act of motherly love, Marie Cooper handed her two-week-old *boppli* over to his brother-in-law, Walter, and made him promise he would keep her safe and give her back when she returned. It seemed like just yesterday when he walked in and saw Stella nursing the English *boppli*.

Chapter 19

The Funeral Sixteen Years Earlier

July 16, 2001
Willow Springs, Pennsylvania

Stella could tell by the position of the sun shining through her bedroom window Jacob let her sleep in. She could hear him rooting around in the kitchen trying to get the *kinner* breakfast. He'd been anxious to get out to the woodshop and knew she must force herself out of bed.

She smiled as she thought about how caring he'd been with her the last few days. This pregnancy was so different from her other two, and she was thankful he'd been so willing to help. She smelled the coffee and knew he was trying to get things started before he came to wake her. It had to be close to seven o'clock and knew he needed to get to work.

She pushed herself up and swung her feet over the side of the bed. Her lower back was aching as she took an extra minute to use both hands to rub the area that was causing her pain. Her due date wasn't until the middle of August and figured she'd overdone it yesterday. She rubbed her stomach and said, "Good morning, little one, it's time to wake up."

The *boppli* wasn't very active this morning, and she figured it must be tired as well. She was now having second thoughts about weeding so much of the garden yesterday, but it had been a beautiful summer day, one she had to take advantage of.

Just as she stood up to get dressed, Jacob walked in, carrying a cup of coffee and greeted her with a warm smile.

"The *kinner* are eating a bowl of oatmeal, and I've fixed myself some toast and coffee. I'm heading out to the shop and will come back in and check on you in a few hours. Can I get you anything before I go?"

"No, I think I'm good. *Denki* for letting me sleep in, I'm not sure why this pregnancy is wearing me out so. I don't remember being drained like this with the other *kinner*," she said as she reached for her hairbrush.

She giggled as she brushed out her long hair and twisted it into a knot to secure it at the base of her neck.

"I guess I didn't have three *kinner* to run after then either."

Jacob leaned down and kissed the top of her head and said, "*Ja*, that's for sure."

As he turned to leave, he heard the front door open and heard Kathryn holler up the stairs.

"Jacob, there's a phone call for you in the shop. The woman on the phone says she's your sister and needs to talk to you right away."

Jacob looked at Stella, and they both knew what the phone call was about. Jacob's *datt* had been ill, and it was only a matter of time when they would be called to go to Sugarcreek for a funeral.

Stella finished dressing while Jacob went to take the call from his *schwester*.

It was times like these when Jacob was glad his bishop allowed him to have a phone in the shop to take orders from the English. He wasn't sure where his *schwester* had gone to make the call, but he didn't want to keep her waiting too long. It only took a couple minutes for him to make his way out of the house and across the yard to the woodshop.

"Hello, Anna Mae, is that you?"

"Jacob, *Datt* passed away last night in his sleep. He's no longer in pain and has gone to be with *Mamm* in heaven. Walter and the boys are preparing things now, and we'll open the house the day after tomorrow for the funeral. Will you and Stella be able to come?"

"Stella is eight months pregnant, but I think if we can get the neighbors to watch the *kinner*, she may want to go just to have a couple days' rest. I have some things to finish today, so we'll leave first thing in the morning if I can secure a driver."

He hung up the phone and headed back to the house to talk to Stella.

Stella knew by the look on his face that they'd been right and the phone call was about his *datt*.

"If we can get Levi and Ruth to watch the *kinner*, are you up for a trip to Sugarcreek in the morning?"

"I'll be fine. I'm not due for a few more weeks, and I certainly don't want you going alone."

"I'll go over to Levi's, call a driver, and then I have a couple orders to finish up, but I'll be back in for dinner. Don't you do too much today!" he ordered as he walked out the door.

Stella started to clean up the breakfast bowls when she had to stop and pull a chair out to sit down. Things in Sugarcreek were always stressful for Jacob. His family felt like he'd abandoned his responsibilities when he ran off to Willow Springs to apprentice with her *datt*. They never understood his love for wood and why he gave up farming. She certainly didn't want him to go to his *datt*'s funeral alone. She rubbed her back again and was sure it was false labor and nothing to worry about.

She only allowed herself to sit a few minutes before she forced herself to get up and finish cleaning the kitchen.

The next morning, Jacob got up early and walked the *kinner* to the Yoder's before the driver was due to pick them up. He was anxious to get to his *schwester's* to help his brother-in-law get things ready for the funeral. He may not have been there to help his *schwester* with his ailing *datt*, but he wanted to be sure he was there in plenty of time to help get things ready for his funeral. When he returned to the house, Stella was sitting at the table with their overnight bag sitting by the front door.

"I see you're all ready to go," he said as he looked at the wall clock. "Our driver should be here any minute. Are you sure you're up for a two-hour ride? You look tired, and you didn't sleep well last night."

"I swear this *boppli* has its feet poking out my back. I can't get it to move from the position it's in. I think the quiet car ride will do us both some good. I may just fall asleep if that's all right with you?"

Just then, Jacob saw their ride turn down the driveway and pull up to the porch. He walked over to where she was sitting and took her hand to help her stand up. With a big smile on his face, he said, "There's nothing as funny as watching a pregnant *fraa* try to stand up by herself."

She gladly took his hand and grabbed her shawl off the peg by the front door.

Jacob guided her down the front steps and into the back seat of the waiting car. He handed the driver the address to his *schwester*'s house and asked him to pop the trunk so he could put the overnight bag inside.

Stella was still trying to find a comfortable position when they drove past the Yoder's. Standing at the end of the driveway all lined up in a row, bare feet, and all in blue, stood Matthew, Samuel, Rebecca, and Anna, waving at them as they passed. Ruth was standing behind them, just as pregnant as she was and waving just as hard.

"Oh, how sweet, I'm going to miss our *kinner*. It was so kind of Ruth and Levi to agree to watch them for us. Ruth is due to have her *boppli* any day now too, and I sure hope she holds on until we get back."

"Ruth's *mamm* is staying with her until she has the *boppli*, and she said she has lots of help and will be okay keeping them for a couple days. Now you just lay your head back and relax and enjoy the peace and quiet."

Stella took Jacob's advice and put her head back on the seat and closed her eyes. She laid her hand on her stomach and thought how strange it was that she hadn't felt the *boppli* move much the last couple days. She figured her time might be getting closer than she thought but decided not to say anything to Jacob just yet.

Jacob and the driver spent the next two hours talking about the weather and everything they passed along the way. He was trying to keep his mind off his *datt*'s funeral. His *schwester* and older *bruders* took on the responsibility of caring for his aging parents, and he felt a sense of guilt for not being in Sugarcreek to help. He was looking forward to seeing Anna Mae and knew Stella was excited to see her as well. They wrote to each other often, and he knew she missed her.

As they approached Troyer Lane, Jacob reached over to lightly shake Stella to wake her.

"It's time to wake up, sleepyhead, we're here."

Stella turned her head toward his voice and smiled. "Already? Oh my, I slept the whole way."

She sat up straight as they turned down the lane that led to Walter and Anna Mae's farm. It was the farm Jacob was raised on; and when he left to go to Willow Springs, Walter and Anna Mae had just married and moved into the *doddi haus*. As his parents got older and Walter and Anna Mae started to have *kinner*, his parents turned the farm over to Walter. By then, Jacob's older *bruders* were all married and had farms of their own. Jacob was the youngest and was expected to take over the farm, but his love for wood sent him to Willow Springs, leaving his family feeling rejected.

Jacob got out of the car and walked around the other side to help Stella out. When he opened the door to reach in to take her hand, she had a strange look on her face.

"What's the matter?"

Stella didn't want to worry him, but she was sure she had just had a contraction.

"I think not moving for the last couple hours has me all cramped up. I just need to get out and walk around for a bit. Help me out and into the house. I need to get a drink of water and some fresh air."

Jacob helped her out of the car.

As they approached the front of the house, Anna Mae heard the car and walked out onto the porch. She waved a friendly hello and walked down the steps to meet them.

"Stella, you look like you're about ready to have that *boppli* any day," Anna Mae said.

"I'm not due until next month. This child is all in front and might be even bigger than Matthew when he was born. The last couple days, I feel like it's kicking me in the back something awful. Jacob thinks it must be a boy for as big as I got this time. The midwife only hears one heartbeat, so it must be just a big one."

Anna Mae took her arm and told Jacob to grab their bag and pay the driver while she got Stella into the house.

As she leaned on Anna Mae and let her carry some of her weight up the stairs, she whispered, "I think I just had a contraction in the car, but I didn't tell Jacob I don't want to worry him. He has enough on his mind right now."

"Well, let's keep that between us for a little bit and make sure they just aren't false pains from riding so long in the car. Come sit in the kitchen with me, and I'll get you a drink."

For the rest of the day Jacob, Walter, and his *bruders* busied themselves with preparing the house for the funeral. A plain wooden box had been delivered, and the men were preparing their *datt*'s body for the funeral. The front room had been set up like a church service, and the casket was sitting at the front of the room. The coffin lid was closed, and the room had an eerie feel to it.

After the women had busied themselves in the kitchen preparing food for the next day, they moved to the front porch and were enjoying a cool breeze as they spent some time visiting with one another. It had been years since they had spent any time together and were thoroughly enjoying themselves, even if it was a funeral that brought them together. Anna Mae looked at Stella when she heard a slight moan escape her lips.

"How long has it been since the last one?"

Stella looked at her watch and said, "Fifteen minutes."

"I think we might have to tell the men you're in labor."

"Not yet, let's wait until after supper and see if they slow down some. Do you mind if I go in and lie down for a few minutes?'

"No, not at all. I'm going to go start supper. Go lie down on my bed, so you don't have to go up all those stairs, and that way I can hear you if you need me for anything. I won't say anything to Jacob right this minute."

Stella stood up, just as Jacob looked her way. He was standing near the barn talking to Anna Mae's five boys and waved at her as she walked to the front door.

Once she made it to Anna Mae's bedroom, she kicked off her shoes and curled up on the bed. She couldn't stop the uneasy feeling she was having about the *boppli* not moving and had decided if the contractions didn't stop by the time supper was finished, she would send Jacob after the midwife to check her. She closed her eyes and fell right to sleep.

Chapter 20

The Boppli

Anna Mae was busy making supper but took a few seconds to walk through the front room to her bedroom to check on Stella. She quietly opened the door and saw that she was sleeping, so she closed it gently and went back into the kitchen. When she called the men and her boys in to eat, they had all sat down before Jacob noticed Stella was not there.

"Where's Stella?"

"She was feeling tired, so I told her to go lie down and that I would wake her when supper was ready. I just checked on her before you came in and she's sleeping. I think we should just let her sleep while she can. Pretty soon, that *boppli* will be keeping her up all through the night, so we might as well let her sleep while she can."

"I shouldn't have brought her. Tomorrow is going to be a long day, and it's going to wear her out."

"She'll be okay. Women have been having babies for centuries, and we're tougher than you all think. I'll check on her again after we've eaten."

They had barely taken a bite when Stella screamed.

Jacob jumped and immediately ran to her, with Anna Mae right behind him. When they got to the bedroom door, Anna Mae stepped in front of him and told him to wait there while she went and checked on her.

"She's been in labor all day and didn't want to tell you until she was sure, but by the sound of it, I would say there's no denying it any longer. I've delivered my share of babies and I think I can handle this without men in my way. Now go finish your dinner, and I will call you if I need you."

Jacob just stood there as Anna Mae opened and closed the door in his face. No matter how many *kinner* they had, the birthing stage always made him nervous.

Walter had walked into the room and stood beside him. He was a man of few words but looked over at the casket that was sitting to his right and said, "*Gott* replaces what He takes away."

He turned and headed back into the kitchen. As he walked away, he hollered over his shoulder, "You might as well come eat. There's nothing we know that can help with birthing a baby, and she'll come get us if she needs something. Best just let nature take its course."

Jacob walked over to his *datt*'s casket and couldn't help but remember how much he enjoyed playing with Matthew the last time they were here. His *datt* loved his grandchildren and was sorry he wouldn't get to meet this one.

In the bedroom, Anna Mae was trying to calm Stella down and get her out of her dress and apron and into a nightgown.

"Something doesn't feel right. I haven't felt the *boppli* move at all today."

"You know some *bopplis* slow down some right before delivery. I'm sure everything is fine. It does look like you're gonna have this *boppli* tonight whether it's time or not. If you'd feel better, I can send Jacob and Walter after the midwife. She only lives a few miles down the road, and it won't take them long to bring her back."

"I think we'd better," she said as she braced herself for another contraction.

"It's only been a few minutes since the last one. We might not have time for the midwife, but I'll go tell them to get her anyways."

Anna Mae went to the door and hollered for Walter to come.

"Since this *boppli*'s a month early, I think you and Jacob better go get the midwife."

Jacob was standing behind him and said, "I'm going in to see her for a minute while you hook up the horse and buggy."

Jacob pushed past Anna Mae and went to Stella's side.

"We'll be right back, so you hold tight. I haven't missed one of my *kinners'* being born yet, and I don't plan on missing this one. We'll only be gone thirty minutes."

"I'm sorry I didn't tell you I was in labor. I guess this little one is anxious to meet you and has plans of his own."

He leaned down to kiss her forehead as he said, "I guess he's a little stubborn just like his *mamm*."

Anna Mae came back in the room and shooed him out the door.

"Now get going, this *boppli* isn't going to wait too long."

Walter wasted no time hitching up the horse and buggy and instructed his boys to start the evening chores. He was already inside the buggy when Jacob came out of the house.

The sun was already starting to set behind the barn, and by the time they headed back, they would need the battery-powered lights to guide them home. As they began down the long lane that led to the road, Jacob noticed lights from a car parked at the end of the lane.

"I wonder what that's all about?"

"Probably someone was driving too close to the ditch again. I've had to help someone get out of that ditch more than once. When it rains, the water comes down that ditch fast, and it's a muddy mess if someone slides into it."

As they got closer to the lights, they could hear a man's voice hollering. They pulled the buggy to a stop when they got close enough to see what was going on. The car was parked on the side of the road next to the mailbox. The trunk was opened, and a tire was lying on the ground. It looked like the car had a flat tire, and they were trying to get it changed.

"Well, it doesn't look like they got stuck, just a flat tire."

Walter slapped the reins gently on the horse's back to get the buggy to move closer. He drove the buggy beside the row of maple trees that lined the driveway. It seemed, the people in the car were oblivious to their presence.

The car was barely off the road, and the passenger side door was opened leaning up against the mailbox. The man had his head in the trunk, hollering something neither of them could make out. The woman shut the front door and went around and opened the back passenger door. She pulled a small boy out and rushed him around to the front of the car. She put her finger up to her mouth as if to tell the boy to be quiet as she pointed to the ditch across the road.

From where they were, they could hear a *boppli* crying. The woman stood at the front of the car until she was sure the boy had gone to the ditch as she instructed. She quickly moved to the opposite side of the car and opened the back door. It looked like she was trying to calm the *boppli* down, when all of a sudden the man came up behind her, grabbed her by the hair, and dragged her to the back of the car.

He pushed her to the ground at the rear tire and hollered at her to change the tire. He took a beer out of the trunk and popped the tab before he started to scream instructions at her. The woman fumbled with the carjack, and the man kicked her to move her out of the way.

"Stupid woman, you're good for nothing. You can't even change a tire. Why I keep you around is beyond me! Shut that screaming kid up, or I'm gonna do it for you!"

She tried to get up to go to the baby when he picked up the tire iron and hit her on the back of the leg.

"Where do you think you're going? I told you to change this tire!" He got the jack in place and jacked up the car then moved out of the way so she could work on changing the tire.

The two men were in shock at what they were witnessing. They had never seen anyone treat a woman so harshly and didn't know what to do.

The man picked back up his beer and stood over her like a hawk. When she didn't do what he told her quick enough, he poked her in the middle of her back with the toe of his boot.

Jacob jumped from the buggy and hollered, "I can't watch this any longer. We've got to do something."

He took off running to the end of the driveway and stopped behind the man.

"Stop that!"

The man picked up the tire iron and turned and swung it at Jacob, hitting him on the side of the face. The brunt force of it knocked him to the ground. His face was turned in the direction of the woman, and he saw her pick up one of the rocks that were around the mailbox as decoration and hit the drunk man over the head.

The man fell to the ground within inches of Jacob's face. He could feel his own face in a puddle of blood as he lay on the ground, looking in the man's opened eyes. Just by looking at him, he knew he was dead. He looked up at the woman, and it was the last thing he remembered before he passed out.

It happened so quickly. Walter didn't even have time to react before the woman hit the man over the head with the rock. She threw the rock down and crawled into the backseat of the car to get the crying baby.

Walter rushed to Jacob's side and felt for a pulse. He turned him over and saw a long gash on the side of his face. He reached into his pocket for his hankie and applied pressure to the wound. With his other hand, he felt for a pulse on the man's neck, lying beside his knee. He knew without even checking that the man was already dead.

When he looked up, he saw the woman standing behind him, holding a baby wrapped in a pink blanket.

"Is your friend okay? Where did you both come from? I didn't even see you."

"I live at the end of the lane, and we were on our way to go pick up somebody."

"Are you all right? He kicked you pretty hard a couple times."

"I'm fine. I'm used to it, and that's nothing compared to how he usually gets when he's been drinking. I have my cell phone. I'll call for an ambulance for your friend. I'm sure the police will need to be called as well."

She stood there, staring at the man lying on the ground. Walter didn't see any emotion in her eyes. She didn't look upset or even sad that the man was visibly dead.

"Is he your husband?"

"If you can call him that, he only comes around when he needs money."

She turned and went to get her phone while Walter tried to keep the pressure on Jacob's face. When the woman returned, she had a blank look on her face and said, "An ambulance and the police are on their way."

Chapter 21

Crying Boppli

A nna Mae had her hands full, trying to keep Stella calm. The contractions were coming one after another, but the *boppli* was not progressing. She knew something was wrong and thought maybe it was breech. She tried to move the *boppli* with her hands on Stella's abdomen like she'd seen the midwife do but wasn't having any luck. She could see that she was fully dilated but still couldn't see the top of its head.

What is taking Walter so long? He should have been back by now, she thought.

She needed the help of the midwife, or they were going to lose this *boppli*.

Stella was exhausted and knew something was terribly wrong. She didn't have this much pain or trouble with her last pregnancy.

When she didn't think she could push another minute, Anna Mae told her to stop.

"I finally see the head. Now we are getting somewhere."

When she told her to start pushing again, it was only a few more pushes, and she held the *boppli*'s head in her hands. The *boppli* was a funny color, and Anna Mae knew something was wrong. With one more push, she knew. The umbilical cord was wrapped around its neck, and she'd not been getting enough oxygen.

Before she could say another word, Stella had pushed the shoulders through, and then Anna Mae was holding the little girl in her hands. She laid the *boppli* down on the bed between Stella's legs and unwrapped the cord from its neck. She felt for a pulse and couldn't find one. When she didn't say anything, Stella cried.

"What's the matter, why isn't he crying?"

Anna Mae just looked up at Stella, and she knew. "The cord—it was wrapped around her neck."

"A girl? Bring her to me."

Anna Mae took a wet washcloth and wiped the *boppli*'s face off, cut the umbilical cord, and wrapped the tiny stillborn in a blanket and laid her beside Stella.

"Where's Jacob? Why isn't he here?"

Stella kissed the top of the *boppli*'s head and cried herself to sleep.

Anna Mae finished cleaning up Stella and gathered the towels and soiled linen and took them to the kitchen. In the distance, she could hear a siren and figured that the men had been held up by an accident somewhere. She prayed for their safe return and sat at the table. It had been a stressful couple of days, and she didn't know how she was going to tell Jacob that he lost his daughter right after losing their *datt*.

She looked up from the table and into the front room. Her *datt*'s casket sat in the dark room as Stella held her stillborn *boppli* girl on the other side of the wall. She didn't understand why *Gott* would call both her *datt* and her niece home all in the same week. What were they going to do? Tomorrow was the funeral, and now they had to plan one for this little girl as well.

When the sirens got louder, she walked over to the kitchen window. She could see the lights at the end of the driveway and immediately got worried.

Did something happen to Walter and Jacob? she thought. *Why are there emergency lights so close to the end of their lane?*

She had to go find out what was going on. Just as she was about to go outside, her son, Martin, came barreling in the front door.

"*Mamm*, do you hear all the sirens? Something must have happened at the end of the lane. We were in the barn doing chores, and we could hear them get louder. *Datt*'s still not back. Should we go see what is going on?"

Just as she was about to tell Martin to run up and see what was going on, Walter walked into the house, holding a *boppli* wrapped in a pink blanket.

"Oh my, Walter, whose *boppli* is that?"

Anna Mae took the *boppli* from his arms as he sat in his chair at the head of the table.

"Where's Jacob? Stella needs him."

By then, all five boys were standing around the table, waiting for their *datt*'s response.

"Walter, where's Jacob?" Anna Mae asked again.

Walter shook his head as he took his hat off and pushed his hair off his forehead.

"She handed me the *boppli* and told me to leave."

"Who gave you the *boppli*? Where's its *mamm*?"

Martin walked over to the window and said, *"Datt*, what's going on at the end of the driveway? Is Uncle Jacob okay?"

"One of you boys go get the buggy. It's tied to the tree at the end of the lane. Don't say a word to anyone. Just go get the horse and come right back. I mean it. Don't say a word to anyone!"

Martin hollered he'd do it and ran out the door.

Walter continued to speak, "She said her mother was too old and sick to take care of her and that I had to take the *boppli* and leave before the police got there. She made me promise to keep her safe and that I would give her back as soon as she came for her. I didn't know what to do, so I ran and hid behind the tree."

"Where's Jacob?" Anna Mae said again.

"He got hurt, but he'll be okay. I stayed hidden until I was sure the ambulance had loaded him up and left. The lights that are up there now are from the police."

"What are we supposed to do with this child?"

"I'm not sure at the moment. All I know is, I promised to keep her safe until she returns."

"How's Stella?"

She was so caught up in Walter's story, she completely forgot to tell him about Stella. Still holding the little girl, who was clearly hungry and starting to cry louder, she proceeded to tell Walter and the boys about delivering Stella's stillborn *boppli*.

"Boys go finish your chores and help Martin with the horse. I need to talk to your *mamm*."

After the boys had left, Walter told Anna Mae what they had seen, how they came upon the car at the end of the driveway with a flat tire and how the man was clearly drunk. He told her how the man didn't think twice about hitting the woman right out in the open. He told her about watching the woman hide the little boy in the ditch and how she took a rock from around the mailbox and hit the man on the back of the head.

He told her how sad and hopeless the woman looked when she handed him the *boppli*. After he'd taken the child, she ran back to the car and retrieved the car seat. She said she didn't want the police to know she had a baby for fear they'd put her in foster care. He explained how he grabbed the car seat with one hand and cradled the *boppli* in the other as he turned and hid behind the tree when the sirens got closer.

"The *boppli* was fussing so much, I needed both hands, so I threw the car seat over the fence along the driveway and figured I'd go get it later."

Anna Mae started pacing with the crying infant.

"I need to find her something to eat. She must be hungry. It's been a long time since we've had *bopplis* in the house, I don't even have any bottles here." She was bouncing the child, letting her suck on her finger when Martin walked in the back door.

"The police officer said I could take the horse back to the barn, but he wouldn't let me take the buggy. He said it was part of a crime scene and I had to leave it there.

"I know you told me not to say anything to them, but they asked me if I knew the name of the Amish man who was in the buggy. I told them Uncle Jacob's name. They said someone would need to go to the hospital they'd taken him to.

"Before I left, I saw them put handcuffs on a woman and put her in the back of one of the police cars. There was a little boy with her, and another officer was taking him in another car. *Datt*, what happened up there?"

Walter stood up and headed to the door.

"Come with me, son, we need to finish up chores, and I need to make sure your *bruders* know whatever happened here tonight is to stay right here on this farm. I need some time to figure out what we're going to do."

While they were talking, Anna Mae had warmed up a cup of milk and was dipping the corner of a towel in it and trying to get the infant to suck on the cloth.

"What about Jacob? Someone needs to go check on him. What am I supposed to tell Stella when she wakes up, and what are we going to do about these *bopplis*?"

"I just don't know yet. Let me get the boys straight about keeping their mouths shut, and then I'll find a driver to take me to the hospital to check on Jacob."

As he was about to go out the door, he remembered, "I have a lamb bottle in the barn. Will that help?"

"I hardly think this little one is strong enough to suck on a lamb's bottle. I'll figure out something."

In all of her years of mothering, Anna Mae never had trouble calming a *boppli* down. But this newborn was apparently hungry. She had to figure out some way to feed her.

Stella woke to the sound of a *boppli* crying and smiled before she opened her eyes. She felt the bundle wrapped in her arms and, in a sleepy state, thought it was her *boppli* needing nourishment. When she opened her eyes and looked down, she remembered, and a deep sadness overcame her. She thought she was still dreaming, but she could swear she still heard a *boppli* crying.

She cocked her head and listened harder. Sure enough, it was a cry she heard. But whose *boppli* did she hear? At the sound of the crying, she felt her milk release from her swollen breasts, and her heart ached to soothe the *boppli*.

After trying everything she could think of, Anna Mae only had one more idea. She needed to get Stella to nurse the hungry child. She quietly opened the bedroom door, but the fussy infant made it hard for her to be quiet. When she opened the door, Stella was awake and looking in her direction.

"I thought it was my *boppli* girl that was crying when I woke up," Stella said.

"Stella, I hate to ask you to do this, but this child is hungry, and I have tried everything I can think of."

"Whose *boppli* is that? Where is her *mamm*?"

"It's a long story and one I'll tell you as soon as we find a way to feed her."

Stella was still holding her own child and hesitated as she looked down at her *boppli*. How could she nurse someone else's child when she hadn't even had a chance to nurse her own? The *boppli* in her arms was not moving, but the *boppli* in Anna Mae's arms was wailing uncontrollably. Anna Mae carried the infant over to the bed and laid her on the opposite side of Stella and then walked to the other side to pick up the still child.

"Please don't take her far."

Anna Mae looked around the room and saw a clothes basket near the window.

"How about I put her in that basket until Jacob gets back?"

Stella watched as the *boppli* she had carried for the last eight months was taken from her and put in the basket. Her heart was broken, and she felt a profound sense of loss when Anna Mae took the little one from her side.

The crying *boppli* needed to be fed. Stella rolled on her side and pulled her nightgown down to expose her nipple for the *boppli* to find. The infant latched on, and Stella cried as she filled the needs of another woman's child.

Chapter 22

Jacob's Scar

When Jacob woke up, he was in the ambulance. The paramedic was trying to get him to answer some questions he didn't understand.

Why is he asking if I know my name and if I know where I am? he thought.

"Yes, I know my name. It's Jacob Byler, and I'm in Sugarcreek."

He reached up to touch his face when the paramedic grabbed his hand and said, "You'd better not do that. You have a nasty gash on the side of your face. It's gonna take quite a few stitches to sew you back up."

Once they got to the hospital, Jacob was wheeled into the emergency room, and the doctor assigned to him assessed the wound that spread from his temple to his chin. With hardly a second look, the doctor told the nurse to set up an operating room and call for a plastic surgeon. He told the nurse it was going to take more than what he could do in the ER.

As he lay on the cold table, he tried to block out all that he had seen. He was sure he'd seen the woman hit the man over the head with a rock but couldn't be sure. He did remember seeing him pull her by her hair and kick her in the back. He couldn't imagine what would possess a man to treat a woman so badly.

All of a sudden, he thought of Stella and the reason he was out on the road. He had to get back to her. She needed the midwife, and he promised her he'd be right back. He tried to get up, but the nurse pushed him back down and tried to get him to lay still. He was adamant that he needed to leave. The nurse called the doctor back in to help her settle him down.

"I need to go back to my sister's house! My wife is about to give birth, and I need to get back to her."

"You're not going anywhere until we get you stitched up."

Walter walked across the backfield in the dark to his English neighbor's house. He didn't want to walk on the road or take the buggy in case the police stopped him. Martin had said that he saw a coroner's car pull up and that a man was lying in the middle of the road, covered in a white sheet. The police had the road blocked in both directions, and he couldn't leave that way, even if he wanted to. It was getting late, and he hated to ask the older gentleman for a ride but knew he had to go check on Jacob.

His neighbor was full of questions and Walter tried not to say anything that might make him believe he was aware of what was going on. All he told him was he had to go check on a friend in the hospital. The old man turned out of his driveway the opposite way of all the commotion at the end of Troyer Lane. There was yellow crime scene tape strung across the end of Walter's driveway, and he hoped everything would be cleaned up and taken away before people started to show up for the funeral in the morning.

Once they got to the hospital, the driver dropped him off at the front door and asked if he wanted him to wait for him. Walter told him it was late and he could go home. He wasn't sure how long he'd be but would call him when he needed a ride back home. The man assured him it would be all right no matter what time he called.

Walter found his way to the emergency room and asked about Jacob. The lady at the reception desk told him that he was upstairs on the surgical floor, and he should go there and wait. She told him she would call up to the nurse's station and say that Mr. Byler's family was waiting when he got out of surgery.

He found his way to the surgical waiting room just as the eleven o'clock news came on the TV. He was the only one in the room and couldn't understand why the television was on with no one watching it. He would never understand the Englishers' fascination with TV. He stood up, looking for the Off button, when the news announcer started their broadcast.

"Reporter Clancy Reynolds is live on the scene at a murder that's taken place deep in Amish country. Officers from the scene have not given us any details, but witnesses report seeing a young woman being arrested. A white male, who has not been identified, is dead. An Amish man who is believed to have seen the murder has been taken to Memorial Hospital in stable condition. Robert, back to you in the newsroom, and we'll keep you posted as more details become available."

Walter reached up and turned off the television as he mumbled under his breath, "Great, just what we need."

He sat down and put his head in his hands while he tried to make sense of everything that had just happened. Deep in thought, it took the nurse a few times calling his name before he looked up and realized she was talking to him.

"Are you Jacob Byler's family?"

"I am. Is he going to be all right?"

"Yes, he is fine. He'll be in recovery for about an hour, and when he wakes up, I'll take you back to see him."

He thanked the nurse and sat back down to wait.

Time went by quickly, and soon, he was being directed to where Jacob was. When he got back to the recovery room, Jacob was sitting up on the edge of the bed, arguing with the nurse that he was going home.

He turned just as Walter walked in the room.

"Good, you're here. Help me find my clothes and take me home."

The nurse spoke up, "The doctor would like him to stay for twenty-four hours, but he's insisting he needs to go home."

Jacob didn't let the nurse finish before he was asking Walter about Stella.

"How is she? Have you seen her? Is she okay?"

"I haven't seen her, but Anna Mae says she is fine."

"And the *boppli*—did she have the *boppli*? Is he okay?"

"You had a girl."

Walter looked at Jacob and didn't know how he was going to tell him about their *boppli* being born stillborn. He just shook his head, and Jacob knew without him saying a word.

He pointed to the bag hanging from the end of his bed. "Are those my clothes?"

The nurse answered yes and knew by the conversation she'd just witnessed that there was no way she was going to talk him into staying for twenty-four hours as the doctor suggested.

"I'll go get the doctor to write you a prescription for pain, and I'll be right back."

"There's no need for that. I won't take them. Just get me anything I need to sign, and we'll be leaving."

"I'm going to call for a ride. I'll be right back," Walter said.

Jacob sat on the end of the bed, trying to put on his pants, when a police officer came in the door.

"Jacob Byler?"

"Yes."

"I'm Detective Shorts from the Sugarcreek Police Department, and I'd like to ask you a few questions, if you're up to it."

"Officer, I don't want to be rude, but I'm not answering any questions you or anyone else may have until I get home and check on my wife. She gave birth tonight, and I must go to her."

"Would it be all right if I stopped by tomorrow and ask you a few questions about what happened tonight?"

"My father died two days ago, and we'll be having his funeral tomorrow. So, no, it won't be a good time. If you'll excuse me, I must leave."

Walter came back in the room, just as the officer handed Jacob his card and told him he would stop by the day after tomorrow.

Jacob caught a glimpse of himself in a mirror as he walked out of the room. They had him bandaged like a mummy, and the throbbing in his jaw told him he would be in pain for a few days. The pain on his face didn't compare to the pain he felt in his heart, knowing his *fraa* had lost their *boppli* girl and he wasn't by her side. All he could think of was getting as far away from the hospital and Officer Shorts as he could.

He was sure the bishops wouldn't permit him to talk to the police anyway. Their nonviolence belief would prevent them from testifying in court or pressing any criminal charges. They didn't dare talk to anyone else until they met with the bishop.

Walter hadn't even had a chance to tell Jacob about the *boppli* the woman handed him but knew he must before they got to the house. As they turned on the road that led to Walter's farm, they could see the lights of the police cars still shining.

"It looks like they still have your driveway blocked. Do you want to just walk through the field from my house again?" The driver asked.

"That's fine."

Walter looked at Jacob and asked, "Are you okay for a little walk?"

"Yes, the fresh air will do me good and will clear my head before I go in and see Stella. Does she know what happened?"

"I'm really not sure what Anna Mae told her. I left pretty quickly, and she had her hands full when I left."

Jacob had a questioning look on his face, and Walter said he would explain on their walk home.

The driver parked the car and told Walter he didn't owe him anything for the ride.

The men thanked him and turned to start their short walk through the field. On the way home, Walter explained about the *boppli* and how he hid behind the tree when the police first got there. Jacob told him he remembered seeing the woman pick up the rock but didn't remember much after that. Walter said that as far as he knew, the police didn't realize they both had been there. He told him about sending Martin to go get the buggy and the police not letting him take it home.

Jacob stopped and grabbed Walter's arm.

"What are we going to do about the funeral tomorrow?"

"Let's just hope everything is all cleaned up and gone by morning. But right now, I'm more worried about getting you back to the house to be with Stella."

As they walked up to the barn, they could see the boys pulling the buggy into the barn without a horse.

"The police came down to the house and told us we could take the buggy to the barn. Since it was dark and the horse had already been put away, we decided we'd pull it ourselves. It looks like they are cleaning things up now. They've been there all night. We were afraid the driveway would still be blocked off when people started to come for *doddi*'s funeral."

"You boys better get to bed. It's only a couple hours until sunrise, and we have a full day in front of us."

Anna Mae had curled up on the sofa in the front room and had fallen asleep for a few minutes while she waited for Walter to come home.

The window behind the sofa was open, and she heard the men walk up on the porch before they came in through the door. She stood up and met them at the door. She gasped and covered her mouth with her hand as she watched her *bruder* walk through the door with his face mostly covered up with gauze.

"It's not as bad as it looks, just forty stitches. How is Stella?"

"She's been asking for you."

He headed to the door of the bedroom and opened the door just as Anna Mae had begged him to wait. She needed to explain something to him before he went in.

"Not now, I need to see my *fraa*."

When he opened the door, he couldn't believe his eyes. Stella was sitting up in the bed nursing a *boppli* wrapped in a pink blanket.

"Oh, Jacob, there you are. What happened to your face? Anna Mae wouldn't tell me anything, and I've been sick with worry."

"Don't worry about me. How are you?"

He walked over to the side of the bed and looked at the infant she held in her arms. The child had fallen asleep while nursing, and she wrapped the blanket around the little girl and laid her beside her and patted the bed so Jacob would sit down.

Jacob pulled her into his arms and let her cry on his shoulder. Anna Mae followed him into the room and picked up the *boppli* and carried her out into the living room as she shut the door behind her to give them time to grieve in private.

"I knew something was wrong before we left home. She wasn't moving much, and I figured I had just done too much in the garden. I should have sent you for the midwife a lot sooner. I'm so sorry, Jacob. I lost our *boppli*."

The anguish in her voice at believing it was her fault shook Jacob. He reached down and held her head in his hands and laid his forehead against hers.

In a whisper, he said, "If *Gott* chooses to take our daughter home before we even got a chance to know her, that was His will. We are not to question His reason—we are just to accept and trust He knows best."

"Where is she?"

She pointed to the clothes basket near the window.

"I didn't want her to leave my side until you got home to see her."

Jacob stood up and stared at the basket under the window. He was hesitant to go but felt he needed to at least see her. He knelt down on the floor and carefully uncovered her head. Her hair was dark, and it felt like soft feathers on his lips as he bent down to kiss the top of her cold head.

After he had run his fingers down the side of her face trying to etch how she looked in his memory, he covered her head back up, wrapped her tight, and picked her up and carried her to the bed. He held the *boppli* close as he sat back down on the bed next to Stella.

"I know what we should do."

Stella listened as he explained what he felt they should do with the *boppli*. He didn't want to have to explain how she died or where the other *boppli* had come from during his *datt*'s funeral. Since this was not their *g'may*, most of these people, they would never see again.

After the funeral, they would talk to the bishop and figure out what they were going to do with the woman's child. But for now, this was the only way he could think of to ease her sorrow with a house full of people. He asked if she wanted to hold her one more time. She shook her head no, saying that she didn't want her last memory of her being how cold she might feel.

He opened the bedroom door and called for Walter to come into the living room. He stopped at the casket and motioned for Walter to open the lid.

With one hand, he took and moved his *datt*'s arm away from his side to make room for the small child to lie in the crook of his arm. He reached for a small quilt that was on the sofa and spread it out over his *datt* to cover up the infant, in case anyone should look inside. He closed the lid, took the fussy *boppli* from his *schwester*'s arms, and carried her back to Stella, closing the bedroom door as he passed through.

Stella moved over in the bed, making room for Jacob to lie down as she reached to take the baby from his arms. She rolled onto her side and pulled the baby close to her chest to let her nurse, as Jacob snuggled up behind her. His jaw was throbbing and had to position his head on the pillow so he didn't put any pressure on the side of his face that hurt. He silently wished he had taken the prescription for the pain medicine the doctor offered earlier. He couldn't help but think the pain of losing a child was so much worse than the pain he felt on his face.

Chapter 23

Elizabeth

Emma sat on the couch next to her *mamm* as she listened to her *datt* explain how he placed their daughter in the casket with his *datt*. She could feel their pain as they recalled the decisions they made to pretend she was their daughter just for the day of the funeral.

"So, my mother never came back for me?"

Stella spoke up to give Jacob a rest.

"We stayed for two weeks after the funeral, and when no one came to claim you, we took you home. Before we left, Walter reminded us again that he had made a promise to your mother that he would keep you safe and return you to her as soon as she came back. We never did find out why the detectives didn't come back to question your *datt* and only found out months later that your mother was sentenced to prison for fifteen to twenty years.

"The letters in the box are all from your mother. She has sent a letter to Anna Mae's address every year for the last fifteen years, including the one we received last week. Last year, there was a story in the Sugarcreek paper telling of three stories of abuse. One of the stories was your mother's.

"In the story, she claimed to have gone to the police to file a complaint just one week before she killed him. The story exposed how the legal system had failed your mother and how the detectives closed the case after claiming they couldn't get any cooperation from the Amish community. Your mother confessed to hitting your father over the head with a rock, but the judge in the case had wanted to make a statement and gave your mother the longest sentence allowed. After the story, a new lawyer took her case and had the conviction overturned. According to the papers, she is due to be released within the next couple weeks.

"We've been so afraid to tell you for fear you'd leave, or worse yet, your mother would come and take you before we had a chance to explain everything. You have to believe, when we brought you back to Willow Springs, we thought we were just keeping you safe until your mother came to get you. The days turned into months, and before we knew it, we were calling you Emma and raising you as our own. In the back of our minds, we knew this day would come—we just didn't know it would be so hard."

Just then, Someday started to bark. The bark startled them, and they all stood up to look out the window. When Emma saw that it was Daniel's truck, she ran to the door and stood on the porch.

Daniel sat in the truck, looking at Emma. Matthew was the first to get out and walked around the truck and stood at the bottom of the steps, looking up at his parents who were standing behind Emma.

"Tell me it isn't true. Have you been lying to all of us for the last sixteen years? Aunt Anna Mae told us a pretty steep story about who Emma really is."

Emma walked down the steps and past her *bruder* as she said, "I'm sure everything she told you was true." She stopped at the side of the truck, reached up, and unpinned her *kupp* and let it fall to the ground. She crossed in front of the truck and climbed in the door Matthew had left open. She didn't look back at her parents but straight ahead and motioned Daniel to leave.

As they drove away, she thought again of her *datt*'s words and knew he was right.

Her life was never going to be the same again...

Epilogue

Daniel stopped the truck at the end of the driveway as he waited for a buggy to pass by. With both hands on the wheel and looking straight ahead he asked, "Do you like ice cream?"

"Yes, my favorite is a sundae with pineapple and caramel from the Dairy Bar in town."

Feeling an instant connection to his sister, even if it was for her love for a caramel sundae, his eyes sparkled as he said, "Me too."

Wringing her hands on her lap and straightening her apron, her voice cracked as she said, "I guess we have more in common than just ice cream."

"That's for sure, and it's about time you heard all about the English family we share."

Her stomach flipped as he referred to her family as English. She had been Amish her whole life and didn't know how to be anything else and, for that matter, wasn't sure if she wanted to be anything else.

As they drove past the Yoder's, she noticed buggies parked in the yard. She remembered that tonight was her first *singeon* and Samuel would be expecting her to be there.

"Have you ever been to a youth gathering?"

"Yes, I've gone to a few when I lived in Ohio. Why do you ask?"

"How would you like to take your *schwester* to her very first one tonight?"

"I'm sure that can be arranged, but how about we go get that ice cream first? We have a lot to talk about."

Daniel pulled his truck into a parking space behind the Dairy Bar and turned in his seat to face her.

"I know this must be hard for you, and I don't want to throw so much at you so fast that you get overwhelmed. I can only imagine you feel betrayed by your parents. But I must tell you they probably saved your life.

"The life I remember as a child was filled with fear and disappointment, which probably is completely different from the life you lived. Your parents protected and shielded you from an ugly world and gave you love and security, something I didn't find until I was adopted."

Putting the palms of her hands to her forehead and resting her elbows on her knees, she let out a deep sigh.

"I'm so confused. What am I supposed to do now? I feel like my life was a lie, and now I don't know who I really am."

"Emma, you're the same person you've always been. The sweet, happy, easygoing Emma who loves to garden, who's a good friend, who makes people smile by just being around you—that hasn't changed."

"But it has. I'm not Emma Byler, I'm Elizabeth Cooper."

"It's just a name. Your name doesn't define who you really are. What defines you is your love for God, your gentle spirit, your eagerness to find the joy in whatever life throws at you. And right now, life's throwing you a curveball."

What's important is how you deal with learning who your biological parents are and why your mother handed you off to a stranger."

"I overheard my *datt* say one time that my life was never going to be the same. I understand now what he meant, but I don't want it to change. I like things just the way they are."

"Boy, are we more alike than I ever thought. When our mother asked me to find you, it took me weeks to come to terms with what she wanted me to do. I said the same thing. I liked my life just the way it was, and I didn't want it to change. But if I remember right, it was you who convinced me that I needed to find my sister. When I left that day, I prayed that if I found her, she'd be just like you. Now isn't that crazy?"

After they'd picked up their orders, they found a seat at one of the picnic tables under the canopy, neither of them said a word for a very long time.

"Who am I? Am I English or Amish?"

"You're neither—you're a child of God. You just happen to be born to an English mother and raised by Amish parents. Please try not to label yourself either way. God has given you life and gives you free will to make your own choices.

"He put this day in your path, and it's your choice to figure out which one you'll follow. No matter if you choose to stay in your Amish community or you want me to help you learn about being English, it doesn't matter. Both worlds revolve around one God."

"I don't mean to be preaching to you, but I want you to understand that God loves you, and it doesn't matter which world you live in as long as you look to Him for guidance.

He shook his head and said, "I sure do need to listen to my own advice. I've lived a better part of my life being mad at her. Maybe God has put us together to help each other with forgiveness. I need to forgive Marie Cooper, and you need to forgive your parents."

"But what should I do about them keeping this from me for so long?"

"You forgive. You've seen firsthand the torment your father's been in. He tried to protect you, just like our mother did when she handed you to a stranger. I didn't think about it before, but think of it this way:

"God put Walter and Jacob in your path for a reason all those years ago. He brought my adoptive parents in my path as a way to save me from a life of disappointment, and now he's brought us together for a reason. Maybe, just maybe, he brought us together to help our mother heal from the life she gave up by protecting us."

"Oh my, after everything I've learned today, I've not once thought about the pain she's been in. She sacrificed her own life to save ours, and I'm selfish, turning my frustration into anger toward my parents. I didn't look back when we pulled away today, but I can only imagine the pain they both felt when I took my *kapp* off and threw it to the ground. What a childish thing to do."

"We both have a lot of forgiving to do but remember we're both human just like our parents are. We all make mistakes and make choices that might not be the best for us. But in the end, if we take our worries and lay them at the feet of Jesus, He will guide and protect us. We need to trust Him that He'll see us through anything life hands us."

Just as they were about to stand, a car pulled in behind them, and a group of small children dressed in blue and black barreled out. The woman driver—Shelby, the local Amish tour guide—had her hands full trying to direct the group of kids to stand in line for ice cream.

"Emma Byler, is that you? It's been years since I've seen you. Look at you all grown up! Where's that little brown-eyed girl that used to run behind my car looking for candy when I brought tours to the furniture shop?"

"It's still me. I'm just not chasing candy anymore."

"Does that mean your chasing boys?"

"Shelby!"

They both giggled and gave each other a warm hug.

"Well, I'd better get these kids the ice cream I promised them. It was so good to see you. Take care and God bless."

Throwing her ice cream dish in the trash, she followed Daniel to the truck.

"Who was that woman?" he asked.

She gives tours and brings English customers to many of the Amish merchants around town. She's been wonderful about bridging the gap between the English and our Amish community.

"It's crazy that the English think we live such a simple life. Shelby helps them understand that we're just like them, and even though our *Ordnung* may direct us to follow *Gott* differently than the English do, we all serve the same—*Gott*. As a child, I remember how we looked forward to her visits. She always had a trunk full of candy to share with us, and she was the first real English person I'd ever met. We taught her some Amish words, and she brought us presents on our birthdays and for Christmas. Life was so simple then."

He opened her door and said, "I've learned life does get a little harder as we get older, but only because we understand we must make our own choices in life. When we're little, we have the protection of our earthly father, but as we get older, we learn we must trust in the protection and guidance of our Heavenly Father."

As she climbed up into the truck, she said, "How did I get so lucky to have such a wise older *bruder*?"

"Oh, believe me, I'm not that wise. I just had a good teacher. My adoptive father is the most loving and caring man a boy could ask for."

She reached up and wiped the corner of her eye with the back of her hand as a flood of memories came back to her.

It was her *datt* who taught her how to fish and picked her up and carried her when a mean rooster backed her in the corner of the porch. It was her *mamm* who nursed her back to health after she got her tonsils out, and it was her *schwesters* who stayed up late telling her all about the *singeons*. It was her *bruder* Matthew who taught her how to ride a horse, and it was Shelby the tour guide who showed her it didn't matter if she was Amish or English if she had a giving spirit filled with *Gott*—that was all that mattered. She owed all of that to her *datt* who protected her just like he had promised to do sixteen years ago.

"Can we stop by my parents' house before we go to the *singeon*? I need to show them I'm okay and let them know that even though I don't know what choice I'll make for my future, I'll always be their daughter, Emma Byler."

Secrets of Willow Springs – Book 2

August 2017

The early morning light had just started to flood the corridor when the seven o'clock bell rang. The steel lock that kept Marie Cooper in her cell slid open, and an armed guard was waiting to escort her to processing. Pushing herself off her bottom bunk, she reached for the small bag at her feet that contained her meager belongings and headed for the door. Stopping only for a second to look back and wave goodbye to her cellmates, she suddenly felt a sense of sadness. These women had become like family, and even though she hated to admit it, she felt closer to them than she did her own.

Walking through the double doors that separated her from the outside world, she was stopped and padded down by two female guards. After passing through to the reception area, she found herself sitting at a desk, listening to the monotone voice of the discharge officer. Signing her name to a form, indicating she understood she could not vote, carry a firearm, or leave the state of Ohio—she laid the pen aside and folded her hands on her lap. Her heart raced as the officer read the date and time she was to report to her probation officer and the monthly amount that would be due in thirty days to pay her fines.

After the officer finished all of the release documents, she directed Marie to move to the counter at the back of the room. There she found herself looking down at the items that had been emptied out in front of her. Listening to the inventory being rattled off by the large woman behind the counter, each piece forced her to remember something she had tried hard to forget.

"One gold band."

Against the wishes of her mother, she ran away with the first boy that paid any attention to her. When the bruises became too hard to conceal, and all of her mother's predictions came true. She cut off all ties with her.

"One pair of jeans and one pink T-shirt."

The blue stretchy material reminded her that she hadn't even gotten a chance to work off her pregnancy weight before being arrested.

"One nursing bra."

Just another reminder that she never got to raise her daughter, and the sound of a baby crying still haunted her dreams.

"One necklace."

At the age of fourteen, after giving her life to Christ, her mother surprised her with the simple gold cross. It was all she had to remember her by now.

The woman pushed another form at her to sign and pointed to the area where she could change out of her prison clothes and into the ones in front of her. She scooped up her belongings and headed to the changing room.

Closing the door with her foot, she leaned back and tried to ward off the tears that were pooling in her eyes. This day was supposed to be happy, but the fear she felt was traumatizing.

Pulling the blue shirt over her head, she caught a glimpse of herself in the mirror. Her golden hair was now showing signs of silver flecks at her temples, and the brown eyes that once had been full of hope and wonder had turned cold and lifeless.

Slipping her legs into the loose jeans, she realized not only had her body changed, everything about her was different. Years in prison had hardened her, and she wasn't sure she liked who she saw in the mirror.

She had failed her children, but more importantly, she felt like she had failed God. She killed her husband in a fit of rage, gave her baby away to a stranger, and signed over her parental rights so her son could be adopted. Her only stability in life had been her mother, and she had long passed away. She had no one who cared or, better yet, no one who loved her. Daniel Miller, her son, was only helping her out of duty, and he'd made it clear he wasn't happy about letting her back in his life. He was her only connection to freedom.

After pushing the gold band in her pocket, she clasped the necklace around her neck and laid her hand over the cross that fell in the hollow of her neck. At one time, the cross meant the world to her, but years of feeling abandoned by God left her full of resentment. No matter how she looked at it or how many prison ministers had tried to reach out to her, she couldn't let go of the feeling of being forgotten by Him.

A hard knock on the door reminded her that she was still under the watchful eye of the guard and she was taking too much time changing her clothes.

Opening the door, she walked past the guard and handed the woman at the desk her neatly folded pile of prison clothes. After the guard asked her a series of questions about who was picking her up and if she understood she had an appointment with her parole officer the next day, she was instructed to sit in the reception area to wait for her ten o'clock release time.

The hands on the clock above the door made a loud click as it reached nine. Again, fear started to take over.

What would happen if Daniel didn't come pick me up? she thought. *Where could I go? How would I get to my appointment tomorrow?*

Her stomach churned as she tapped her fingers on the wooden arms of the chair. *That voice—there it is again.*

She closed her eyes and tried to get it to leave her head. It was getting louder and louder, and no matter how hard she tried to push the words away, the whispers kept coming. Deep down, she knew who it was, but she wasn't ready to listen.

"Do not be terrified, do not be discouraged, for the Lord your God will be with you wherever you go."

She shook her head, trying to quiet the small voice.

Where have I heard that before? Was it one of the Bible verses Mother often read to me, or was it a Sunday school memory verse playing in my head?

Wherever it was, she knew she needed to put her trust in God, but years of torment left her feeling that she could count on only one person—*herself.*

Picking up the bag at her feet, she peered inside, making sure she had everything with her. *Is this all I have to show for thirty-nine years?*

She pulled the ring from her pocket and put it in the bag as she picked up the torn and tattered picture of a baby. There was no way for her to know what Elizabeth looked like or even how she'd spent the first sixteen years of her life. The unanswered letters she'd sent to the address where she'd left her gave her no hope. She begged Daniel to visit the address in Sugarcreek to see if he could find his sister, but she had not heard if he had gone.

Aside from the picture, she had a few short letters from Daniel that were anything but casual at best. She owned a brush, a toothbrush, and a picture of her mother. What fond memories she had of her mother. It didn't matter that her father had died when she was five, her mother worked to support them both and always made it a priority to raise her in a good Christian home.

How was she ever going to face it all without her mother by her side? She felt all alone in a world that had shown her no mercy. Harshly sentenced for a crime by a judge who was out to use her as an example and married to a man who used her as a punching bag, life as she saw it was hopeless.

The room was cold and lifeless just like her cell had been, and she was anxious to leave the bitterness behind. How was she ever going to ward off these dark feelings? Sitting on the stand beside her was a leather-bound Bible. Instantly, her hand was drawn to it. Instead of opening it up, she laid her hand on top of it. Memories of the well-worn pages of her mother's Bible flashed in her head. A warm feeling passed through her hand, and she jerked it away as if she'd touched something hot.

"Cooper."

Startled by the buzz that unlocked the door, it took her a minute to realize her name had been called, and the door swung open.

Standing on wobbly legs, she passed the guard seated at the entrance. Without looking up, he instructed her that her ride was waiting in the parking lot near the front security checkpoint.

Stepping outside, she closed her eyes and raised her face to the sun. It felt warmer, and the air seemed fresher than it had ever felt before. A dragonfly fluttered in front of her nose and made her smile. The first real genuine smile she'd had in years. For a moment, chills ran down her arms and warmth surrounded her like someone had embraced her in a loving hug. One single tear rolled down her cheek as she pushed the feeling away and shook her head back to reality.

Focusing her eyes toward the security gate, she saw a man, not the boy she'd left behind. Daniel was leaning up against his truck, his arms folded tightly across his chest. Her heart ached to hold him close and tell him how sorry she was. He'd been through so much because of the choices she'd made. How was she ever going to mend his broken heart?

Books by Tracy Fredrychowski

The Amish of Lawrence County Series
Secrets of Willow Springs - Book 1

Secrets of Willow Springs - Book 2

The Women of Lawrence County

Join the Amish Readers Club and get 10 recipes from the
Women of Lawrence County
https://tracyfredrychowski.com/sweettreat/

The Apple Blossom Inn Series
Love Blooms at the Apple Blossom Inn

What did you think?

First of all, thank you for purchasing **Secrets of Willow Springs –
Book 1**. I know you could have picked any number of books to
read, but you picked this book and for that I am extremely grateful.
I hope it added value and quality to your everyday life. If so, it
would be really nice if you could share this book with your friends
and family on Social Media.

If you enjoyed this book and found some benefit in reading it, I'd
like to hear from you and hope that you could take some time to
post a review on Amazon, BookBub or Goodreads. Your feedback
and support will help me improve my writing craft for future
projects.

Glossary of Pennsylvania Dutch "Deutsch" Words

Ausbund. Amish songbook.
boppli. Baby.
bruder. Brother
datt. Father or dad.
denki. "Thank You."
doddi. Grandfather.
doddi haus. A small house usually next to or attached to the main house.
fraa. Wife.
g'may. Community.
haus. House.
ja. "Yes."
kapp. Covering or prayer cap.
kinner. Children.
mamm. Mother or mom.
mei lieb. "My love."
mommi. Grandmother.
mun. Husband.
nee. "No."
Ordnung. Order or set of rules the Amish follow.
rumshpringa. "Running around" period.
schwester. Sister.
singeon. Singing/youth gathering.

The Amish are a religious group that is typically referred to as Pennsylvania Dutch, Pennsylvania Germans or Pennsylvania Deutsch. They are descendants of early German immigrants to Pennsylvania and their beliefs center around living a conservative lifestyle. They arrived between the late 1600s and the early 1800s to escape religious persecutions in Europe. They first settled in Pennsylvania with the promise of religious freedom by William

Penn. Most Pennsylvania Dutch still speak a variation of their original German language as well as English.

Appendix

Melt-in-Your-Mouth Amish Sugar Cookies

1 c. powdered sugar
1 c. sugar
1 c. unsalted butter, softened
1 c. canola oil
2 tsp. vanilla
2 eggs
5 c. unbleached all-purpose flour
1 tsp. salt
1 tsp. baking soda
1 tsp. cream of tartar

Preheat oven to 350° F.
In a large bowl, cream together sugars, butter, canola oil, vanilla and beat until light and fluffy. Add eggs one at a time and blend evenly. In a separate bowl, sift together the flour, salt, baking soda, and cream of tartar. Gradually add flour mixture to wet ingredients until combined.
Drop rounded 2-inch balls on an ungreased cookie sheet.
Flatten balls with the bottom of a glass dipped in sugar. Bake for 10 to 12 minutes, until edges turn golden brown. Allow cookies to cool on cookie sheet for 2 minutes before transferring to a wire rack.

About the Author

T racy Fredrychowski lives a life similar to the stories she writes. Striving to simplify her life, she often shares her simple living tips and ideas on her website and blog at https://tracyfredrychowski.com.

Growing up in rural northwestern Pennsylvania, country living was instilled in her from an early age. As a young woman, she was traumatized by the murder of a young Amish woman in her rural Pennsylvania community, and she became dedicated to sharing stories of their simple existence. She inspires her readers to live God-centered lives through faith, family, and community. If you would like to enjoy more of the Amish of Lawrence County, she invites you to join her in her Private Facebook Group. There she shares her friend Jim Fisher's Amish photography, recipes, short stories, and an inside look at her favorite Amish community nestled in Northwestern Pennsylvania, deep in Amish Country.

Follow her at:

Instagram - https://www.instagram.com/tracyfredrychowski/
Facebook - https://www.facebook.com/tracyfredrychowskiauthor
FB Group https://www.facebook.com/groups/tracyfredrychowski/